## Something wr...

O'Neill took his time walking back down to the square, trying to figure out why his feeling of unease was growing with every step. It wasn't as if he was being followed—he was all too familiar with that sensation. There was something else ... he just couldn't put his finger on it.

Everything was exactly the same as when they had arrived. Maybe it was just the unusual circumstance of arriving in the middle of a busy town. After all, how often had the Goa'uld put gates and all their associated technology right in the middle ... ?

Associated technology.

O'Neill spun, searching, a cold chill in his gut. Gate. Platform. Shops. Everything where it should be, except—

*Where was the Dial-Home Device?*
*Uh-oh.*

# THE PRICE YOU PAY

## A Stargate SG-1™ Novel

## Ashley McConnell

Based on the story and characters created by
Dean Devlin & Roland Emmerich

Developed for television by
Jonathan Glassner & Brad Wright

A ROC BOOK

ROC
Published by New American Library, a division of
Penguin Putnam Inc., 375 Hudson Street, New York, New York 10014, U.S.A.
Penguin Books Ltd, 27 Wrights Lane, London W8 5TZ, England
Penguin Books Australia Ltd, Ringwood, Victoria, Australia
Penguin Books Canada Ltd, 10 Alcorn Avenue, Toronto, Ontario, Canada M4V 3B2
Penguin Books (N.Z.) Ltd, 182–190 Wairau Road, Auckland 10, New Zealand

Penguin Books Ltd, Registered Offices:
Harmondsworth, Middlesex, England

First published by Roc, an imprint of New American Library, a division of Penguin
Putnam Inc.

First Printing, July 1999
10  9  8  7  6  5  4  3  2  1

Author's Note: The action in this book takes place approximately midway through Season One of the series.

Special thanks to Robert Cooper, who caught several errors on my part, and to Jonathan Glassner. Any errors which still exist are, obviously, strictly the fault of the author.

This book is dedicated with great conviction to Bildair's After Glow, sine qua definitely non.

# CHAPTER ONE

Jack O'Neill pinched the bridge of his nose and sighed, leaning back in the gray chair and shoving himself away from the metal desk. He had to admit that Devorah Randolph was good at logistics, even though the Major had never been on a Stargate mission herself. Once a new Gate had been located and a probe sent through, Randolph would set to work, taking whatever data on terrain, weather, flora and fauna were available and planning supplies and weaponry as appropriate. She was particularly gifted at learning from past missions and applying those lessons to future ones.

Flora—O'Neill skimmed the consumables list again. Yep, there it was: three boxes of tissue for Daniel Jackson, whose allergies seemed to be triggered by Gate travel. O'Neill could tell they hadn't invented an antihistamine for wormholes yet because Randolph hadn't included any on the supply list.

Randolph kept hinting that if only she could go along on a mission sometime, she'd be ever so much more efficient at the supply business. She seemed to think that the Stargate missions were Great Adventures and that she was missing out on all the fun. O'Neill thought back on some of the "fun" and grimaced. One of these days he was going to take her up on it, but then they'd probably need a new Logistics Officer in short order.

Stargate missions weren't "fun." They were necessary

reconnaissance to ensure Earth's survival in an undeclared war against the Goa'uld, a race of parasitic aliens who had established—or borrowed, or stolen—the Gate technology to make travel between worlds easier by opening wormholes between predetermined coordinates. Thousands of years in the past, one of the Goa'uld had set a Gate in ancient Egypt and used it as a base to kidnap humans and seed them all over the galaxy. The Goa'uld liked to think of themselves—and have humans think of them—as gods. They had adopted much of ancient Egyptian mythology along with their human hosts.

But that had been long ago. Eventually both humans and Goa'uld had forgotten the existence of the Earth Gate, until it was rediscovered by archaeologists. The Gate had been moved to a site in the U.S. at Cheyenne Mountain, and almost by accident they'd found a sequence of symbols that jolted the ancient Gate back into operation. That had led, in turn, to the planet Abydos, and a pitched battle in which one of the most powerful Goa'uld, Ra, had been killed.

One of Ra's rivals had decided that this upstart Earth needed to be brought back to heel. Ever since, the Stargate Project had conducted a topmost-secret effort to prepare for an inevitable confrontation. Earth had managed to safeguard its own Gate by installing an iris shield, which had to be opened separately—anyone, or anything, attempting to use the Gate without sending the proper signal would find itself splatted against the shield.

Meanwhile, nine Stargate teams, made up of the best of the best from all U.S. military services, used some of the most powerful computing hardware in the world to calculate the proper sequence of signals to find new Gates and new worlds. The formal mission of the Stargate teams was "to perform reconnaissance, determine threats, and if possible make peaceful contact" with as many worlds as possible.

In fact, the Earth teams went through the Stargate searching for allies, for weapons, for intelligence about the alien race. As the senior officer with the most experience with the aliens, Colonel Jack O'Neill commanded SG-1. It was his responsibility to keep his team safe, to accomplish the mission and get everyone home in one piece. And to do that he had to make sure they had enough weapons, blankets, and Kleenex.

It was so much easier just to shoot at problems . . .

And this new world, like all the rest, presented special problems of its own. The Stargate teams had found Gates in a lot of out-of-the-way places, on worlds that had forgotten their very existence; they'd found them set up as shrines, or remade as triumphal arches. O'Neill allowed himself to contemplate painting a Stargate bright yellow and asking the Goa'uld if they wanted fries—he shook his head. It was really getting late.

The Gate on the world designated NPR76309, however, appeared to be squarely in the middle of a lively town marketplace. The probe had come through the Gate at the other end of the latest set of coordinates only to see buildings, people, animals, all staring at it in bemusement.

It made, as Patton might say, an interesting technical problem.

Ideally, O'Neill preferred to do reconnaissance of new, possibly hostile places from a nice safe distance—say, a space satellite, or at the very least a tall mountain miles away—not from the middle of the sales floor. It was sort of hard to execute both discreet intelligence-gathering and a grand entrance. The Stargate teams could field a lot of manpower these days for the grand entrance part, but there went your discretion factor all to hell and gone.

Made for a challenge, all right.

O'Neill shoved himself back from the table and pinched the bridge of his nose again. He was tired. He'd been working late, and he was wondering if maybe he ought to have a bad feeling about this one. Or maybe he'd be better off saying the hell with it and catching some sack time.

Sometimes it was just more convenient, the night before a Gate jaunt, to stay in quarters in the guts of the mountain. Officers' quarters were cramped, containing only a cot covered with a greenish-gray wool blanket, a metal desk with a lamp and a computer terminal, and a chair. A closet at one end of the room, a tiny bathroom, and a television set tuned more or less permanently to CNN completed the suite.

Oh, all right, he did have an actual office. But it reminded him too much of Hammond, flying a desk, to spend any time working there.

George Hammond, the general commanding the multi-service base in the depths of Cheyenne Mountain, wanted him to take SG-2 along for this one, because of the unique circumstances. Daniel Jackson was appalled at the very thought. For once Jack found himself agreeing with the (relatively, anyway) little archaeologist. SG-2 was a team used for very military encounters, the kind of guys you expected to find walking around the base with Special Forces knives between their teeth, grunting their salutes. Appearing in the middle of a peaceful marketplace with a squad of mixed military types, all lusting for a fight, just didn't feel right. (As long as it really was a peaceful marketplace. Appearances could be, well, deceiving.) SG-1, on the other hand, was himself, Daniel Jackson, Captain Samantha Carter—specialty astrophysics, which made her more of a scientist than a soldier in O'Neill's not-unbiased opinion—and Teal'C, who came from offworld. There were only four of them. SG-1 did mostly science and culture stuff.

They also sometimes carried knives between their teeth, but that was just the nature of the job.

He tapped the touchpad on his keyboard and studied the data from the probe one more time. Daniel said the level of

technology for this place looked like maybe early technological on Earth—they had some nice stone architecture,
fairly sophisticated textiles, iron weapons but no per-
cussion weapons were visible. Daniel had spent years
studying the Stargates, both on Earth and on Abydos. His
background was in ancient archaeology and alien anthropology, insofar as anyone could be said to be an expert in
alien anthropology. But he had unique knowledge, the necessary clearances to work on the project, and he said he
saw nothing that could begin to stand up to a standard
sidearm and no indication that this culture was at that level
of development.

All right, it wasn't very much data, and the lens had
been obscured more than once by the noses of little kids
trying to figure out what the probe was. The first couple of
times that had happened the intelligence analysts had
freaked out. They couldn't recognize the noses on the
faces. After all, how often would an Iraqi kid press his
nose up against a lens on a piece of alien machinery?

So, Daniel had argued earnestly, those noses were data
too; they indicated a reassuring level of curiosity and lack
of fear. Maybe that meant there weren't any Goa'uld on
this new world.

Teal'C hadn't commented on that. Jack still wasn't sure
whether the Jaffa warrior knew anything about this world
or not. Jack had kept an eye on him when the whole team
had reviewed the tapes, and Teal'C had looked grim and
foreboding as the images flashed on the big screen in the
briefing room. Unfortunately, Teal'C *always* looked grim
and foreboding. He hadn't volunteered any comments
during Daniel's preliminary analysis, though, and the big
man would have, if he'd thought the team needed to know.
Teal'C had served the Goa'uld as a very high-ranking
guard and soldier until he finally became convinced that a
race existed that might be able to successfully challenge
them. He also carried the larva of a Goa'uld within his

body, serving as a living example of the threat the aliens represented.

*Once more into the breach, dear friends. . . .* Once more, and once again.

O'Neill sighed. Time to get serious about this. All right, so assume that Jackson won the day, and it *was* just the four of them, Jackson, Teal'C, Carter, and himself. Sidearms, definitely. Rations?

Could they assume they could find food and shelter in this place? Sure, it was a city, and they could bet that the inhabitants were just as human as they were, originally from Earth itself. No problems with food, then, or air. It would be a distinct advantage to travel light, but they might have to pitch a tent in the middle of the town square. If they were ridden out of town on a rail they might need more than that. He scribbled some notes in the margin, looked at the data summary again, and swung around to the keyboard. Moments later a concise request was winging its way to Supply.

A glance at the clock showed 2300 hours. He thought about stepping over to the bar they called the Officers' Club to see who else was up, but decided not to. He wasn't as young as he used to be. Before venturing out to strange new worlds, he'd have to get a good night's sleep. Who knew when he would have another chance?

Elsewhere in the depths of the hidden mountain base, Samantha Carter stared upward, counting the shadowy dots of the acoustical tiles on the ceiling by the green glow of the nightlight in the bathroom. The dots blurred together, and she squeezed her eyes shut.

She could never sleep the night before a mission. The idea of stepping through the Gate, traveling through the chill depths of space to pop out the other side millennia of light-years away, was still hard to believe no matter how many times she did it. O'Neill never seemed affected by it at all, as if it wasn't any more fantastic than taking a flight to New York.

Jackson didn't seem affected by the traveling part either, though he was always intrigued by the unusual and sometimes bizarre twists in human culture that they found on the other side. He was too eager to find his lost wife, Sha're, to spare time for wonder about wormholes he didn't have the math for anyway.

Teal'C—well, Teal'C had been traveling through Stargates since he was a child, and to him there wasn't anything wonderful about them. He was looking for a way to defeat the Goa'uld, and nothing else mattered.

But for herself, the concept of stepping, or perhaps falling, across space was still fabulous, and every night before a mission she lay awake, testing the delicious fear that maybe this time the mysterious technology of the Stargate wasn't going to work.

If it didn't work, what would happen? Would they freeze, human snowballs spinning in space, compressed molecules never to be reconstituted? Or would they be in some other dimension entirely, maybe aware of being lost for eternity? She had a doctorate in astrophysics, and a vivid imagination—never a good combination for an assignment like this one.

She'd always wanted to go into space. Now, at not yet thirty, she had bypassed mere rocketry and walked on alien worlds.

In her off-hours, when she wasn't on a mission, preparing for a mission, or recovering from a mission, she spent her time studying the Stargate, trying to understand the physics of wormholes. Let O'Neill take care of the military stuff; he was good at that. She'd take the science every time. The possibilities were endless.

Tomorrow she was going to step through emptiness

again, fall between the stars to a brand-new world. And it was terrifying, incredible, and wonderful.

And the math of it was beautiful.

Daniel Jackson dreamed.

In his dreams, Sha're smiled at him.

Sha're, his love. His life. His wife.

They were on Abydos again, her homeworld, in their own place, the place that had taken him in and welcomed him and made itself his home too.

Her eyes were dark and lovely, her lips parted. He could smell her perfume, feel the touch of her fingers against his skin, and in his sleep he moaned and twisted against the mattress. She loved him, and he would never stop glorying in the wonder of that love, never stop feeling unworthy of it.

She breathed lightly in his ear, and his breath came short, and he turned to respond to her, to her beautiful eyes and tantalizing touch, to the warmth of her body and soul. Her lovely dark eyes glimmered in the firelight. Her eyes . . . glowed.

And glowed.

Brighter, and brighter.

Until they weren't dark anymore but pits of liquid metal, too hot for mortal eyes, and recognition died in them. The warmth of her touch turned to a terrible heat that pushed him away. Her lips closed; her face was wiped of all expression, as if she had turned to stone, and he felt himself pushed away, falling.

Falling, as she receded from him, slipped out of his arms, away from him, smaller and smaller into the darkness until all that was left of her was the shine of glowing eyes and the terrible lonely echo of his voice calling her name.

"And the top ten reason why Madonna isn't Queen of the World is . . ."

A furrow wrinkled the golden symbol, the Snake enclosed in a royal cartouche, marking him as the personal property of the Goa'uld Apophis, imprinted on Teal'C's forehead. The reasons made no sense. "Virgins don't have enough votes"? "Royalty wears its underwear on the inside"?

Perhaps O'Neill would explain.

On the other hand, often O'Neill made no sense either.

It was, in the phrase of another bald person whom Teal'C had never heard of, a puzzlement. This Earth was a very strange world indeed.

Despite O'Neill's insistence that the people of Earth loved peace and freedom, he could see the very opposite in their "news" broadcasts every night: they had wars, murder, starvation, disease. The Jaffa had none of those things.

But every misery that Earth had, it inflicted upon itself; it was the source of its own problems and therefore held the hope of curing them. The people of Earth were not forced to worship alien parasites as gods, nor were they compelled to host those parasites within their own bodies. None of Earth's peoples surrendered mind, personality, their very souls to Goa'uld, leaving only their bodies as shells and puppets to be manipulated by the aliens, abused and tossed away when they no longer served the alien purpose.

And Earth had honorable men who believed in freedom, in the right to make their own mistakes and find their own solutions. They were willing to fight for that right; they had the hope and the desire and the will to win, and a glimmer of understanding of high technology. That was what he required of his allies. It might not be enough, but it was the best beginning he'd seen so far.

Next to all that, who cared if Madonna was Queen of the World?

# CHAPTER TWO

They stepped through the Stargate on NPR76309 to find
hundreds of people crowded around the alien Gate, gaping
at them.

As marketplaces went, it wasn't bad. It was a large,
open area paved with cobblestones. Low places puddled
with water showed decades of wear as well as a recent
rainstorm. The Gate was on a raised, three-step platform at
one end, and a long street maybe fifteen feet wide led off
the other. The square was defined by the one-and two-
story flat-topped stone buildings surrounding it, fronted by
shops shaded by colorful cloth awnings. O'Neill could see
the usual assortment of goats and radishes, fried foods and
copper bowls and stacks of frangible pottery.

Not Nordstrom's, certainly, but it had a nice variety and
a lot of customers, even though nobody was buying anything at the moment—too busy staring. Not only in the
square, but standing at the open windows and porches of
the buildings, even perching on the roofs, looking over low
walls and down at the unexpected visitors.

Well, it wasn't as if they didn't have some warning.
When the Stargates activated, the sound and fury was
pretty unmistakable.

O'Neill stood at the top of the stone platform and sur-
veyed the crowd, sternly repressing the urge to say, "I suppose you're all wondering why I've called you here

together today . . ." The crowd looked back as if they expected him to say it, too.

As it was apparent that they weren't going to fling themselves upon his team, howling for blood, he allowed himself some more time to look around and orient himself. It was an uneasy look, distracted by the pressure of the stares upon SG-1. There was the probe, tilted over on one side, with a couple of scratches on the surface but no immediately apparent damage. They'd have to remember to take it back with them.

The city resembled ancient Athens, with its white stone, columns, trees, and open spaces. The main street leading off the square dipped down and then led up about a mile to a building whose row of outer supporting columns looked very much like the Agora, the heart and soul of ancient Greek cities, where politics and philosophy and the birth of democracy took place. They would call the place Athenaeum, O'Neill decided in executive fashion. He'd make a note of it.

The people were dressed in colorful tunics both striped and solid, with elaborate hems or none at all, tied at the shoulders and falling to knee-length, their feet either bare or wrapped in leather sandals. Broad belts tied the tunics at the waist, with fringed ends hanging nearly to the ground, and some of the men wore woven, tasseled caps of red and blue and white—now that part looked more Turkish than Greek, somehow. No one looked either excessively poor or excessively wealthy, and he couldn't spot any beggars or cripples in the crowd. That alone was unusual.

But nobody ever said human social evolution had to be absolutely consistent. The weather was mildly Mediterranean too. A soft breeze blew the smells of the goats away. It was humid but not hot, the sun shining almost blindingly on the white stone of the nearby buildings. A few clouds could have been reflections of the city. One or two broken columns and cracked walls simply gave the place character—he found himself looking for souvenir sellers. There might actually be some under the striped awnings, propped with thin sticks against the pavement, that shaded merchants and their customers.

The city itself was set in a kind of bowl, maybe a caldera. The broad street that rose up to the Agora building could have continued beyond it to the brown, rocky hills, spotted with more trees, that defined the horizon. The difference between the trees in the hills and the ones in the city was striking, as if rain ran off the surrounding area and concentrated here to feed the thirsty vegetation. Not a very defensible location; the field of fire from those surrounding hills would be as focused as the rainfall. They were sitting ducks if anyone decided to lay siege to the place.

"They're not scared," Jackson, peering around from behind him, said.

It was true. The Athenians were startled to see them, obviously; the rapid conversations springing up here and there were proof of that. But they weren't afraid. They were staring at the newcomers, talking softly and nudging each other, taking several hesitant steps forward. It was almost as if someone or some ones had been expected, but not so soon.

Which did not bode well for this planet, given what usually came through Stargates, O'Neill thought grimly.

At the same time, whoever was expected, it obviously wasn't three men and a woman dressed in green-tan-and-black-splotched heavy cotton and combat boots, carrying backpacks and rifles.

"Are they going to understand us this time?" he asked, keeping his voice low.

"No telling until we try," Carter answered. "We haven't figured out yet how the Gates affect our ability to speak or understand languages. Sometimes it works, sometimes it doesn't."

"We come in peace," Daniel said, raising one hand and stepping forward.

O'Neill rolled his eyes. Scientists!

"That is not wise," Teal'C muttered.

"When did that ever stop him?" O'Neill asked.

"Never." Teal'C hadn't quite got the knack of rhetorical questions yet.

The people in the marketplace milled around, nudging each other, trying to find a spokesman to deal with this camouflage-clad set of apparitions manifesting through their Gate. Finally a middle-aged woman dressed in reds and browns, balancing a large woven basket full of vegetables on her hip, stepped forward, looking up at them from the base of the stone platform.

"Who are you? Are you Rejects?"

"Well, that answers one question, anyway," Carter said. "I guess we can understand each other without a translator this time. That's convenient."

"We're—we're friends. My name is Daniel Jackson," Jackson said. Then, over his shoulder to the rest of the team, "Are we rejects?"

"Never been rejected in my life," O'Neill responded, sotto voce. As expected, Carter glared at him.

"What is a Reject?" Teal'C asked, frowning. His deep voice carried across the crowd. As he stepped forward, some of the natives spotted the mark, gold lines within a gold oval, embedded in the skin of his forehead. They pointed and whispered, clearly recognizing it.

But they still weren't afraid. It didn't make sense. How could they know the mark of the Serpent Guards and not be afraid of what it meant?

Daniel, exhibiting his usual finely honed sense of self-preservation, was halfway down the platform, peering earnestly through his glasses at the woman who had spoken. "I'm sorry," he was saying. "We don't understand. What are Rejects?"

"Those who return," the woman answered, baffled at his failure to grasp the obvious. "Who are you? Where do you come from?"

Daniel sneezed, and the woman stepped back, startled. "Sorry," the archaeologist apologized. "It's just allergies. We're from Earth."

The word meant nothing to the natives.

"They must have been taken long ago," Daniel said over his shoulder. "They don't know Earth."

"Maybe they just never called it that," Carter pointed out.

"Yeah, you ask me, I'm from Chicago," O'Neill said. Teal'C frowned at him again.

"Could you, er, take us to your leaders?" Daniel had redirected his attention to the woman in front of him, missing O'Neill's groan of disbelief—not untinged by jealousy at having been beaten to it—entirely and probably deliberately.

The woman stared up at them thoughtfully, with special attention to Teal'C. "Our Council is busy preparing for the celebration," she said. "We didn't expect anyone so soon. If you are sent by the Goa'uld, they will want to speak to you immediately, of course."

"*Sent* by . . ." Daniel began, aghast.

"We want to speak to them," O'Neill said sharply, asserting his authority. "As soon as possible." He stepped down off the platform and looked around, one hand resting casually on his sidearm. "Can you take us to them, please?"

Some of the natives were impressed by his presence and bearing. The middle-aged woman wasn't. She looked him up and down, her mouth twisted in doubt, and then shrugged. "Very well," she said, hefting the basket. A younger man came forward and took it from her, staring curiously at the newcomers.

"What's your name?" Carter asked the woman, following O'Neill down the steps.

Jackson winced.

O'Neill sighed, figuring they were going to get the standard cultural touchy-feely lecture as soon as they were alone: if the woman hadn't volunteered her name in response to Daniel's, there was probably some taboo or something that prevented her from providing it, and asking was too, too rude.

"Yeah, what *is* your name?" the colonel asked.

"Atena," the woman said unwillingly.

Atena. Athenaeum. Clearly it was meant to be.

"What do you call this place?" he asked as they made their way through the crowd pressing around them.

"M'kwethet," she responded.

"Gesundheit." Damn. Athenaeum would have been a much better name. The woman looked at him blankly, and he shrugged, smiling. Atena looked away, as if the rules of politeness forbade her from asking for an explanation of that bizarre word. Apparently whatever translated English didn't do the same for German.

Atena led them down the main street out of the marketplace, directly toward the building lined with tall, graceful columns that O'Neill stubbornly insisted on thinking of as the Agora. The others in the marketplace watched them, still murmuring among themselves. The team strode along quickly, observing the porches overhanging the street, the glimpses of life through open windows and doors. There were more shops along this street, but there were also old men and women sitting in the sun, gabbling and pointing at them as they went. Some called out questions to Atena, which she ignored with lofty dignity.

In a few minutes they arrived at the broad porch and stood within the row of columns in the shade. The columns, at least thirty feet tall, sent stripes down the sunlit marble. One or two of the natives exchanged greetings with Atena, sending the visitors curious but unthreatening looks.

Here, too, the elders sat, some playing a game that looked like three-handed chess, some merely gossiping. Three or four young children sat in a rough semicircle before one old man, listening attentively as he read to them from a scroll held open on his lap.

Daniel, of course, paused to check out the architecture, probably identifying it as Ironic or Dori or some such. At O'Neill's summoning glance, Carter hustled him up the steps after the rest of them, to the shaded portico. "This is kinda a nice place," Daniel said, looking around.

"It seems so," Teal'C agreed gravely. O'Neill blinked. It wasn't often that Teal'C agreed to any such thing.

Still, he didn't feel that icky prickling at the nape of his neck. The sunlight was warm, the shade cool, the air—at least now that they were away from the goats—clean and fresh and sweet. He couldn't hear any shouts of alarm or anger anywhere.

Really, it was too good to be true. Something was missing. Where was that familiar cozy feeling of dread and doom?

He thought about it for a moment and decided it really was present after all; he just couldn't figure out what was triggering it. Yet.

Atena, who was the closemouthed type, led them through a high, arched portal into a large inner chamber currently lined with low tables and benches. A number of other doorways at the far end of the hall indicated that the building was considerably more extensive than this single room, large and cheerful though it might be. Light poured in through tall, broad windows that opened out onto the front portico. Children aged anywhere from six to the mid-teens scurried about, arranging sweet-smelling branches and setting fresh torches into sconces, climbing up ladders to put not-quite-sheer drapes in place to cover the plain walls. Now that they were completely out of the sunlight, the temperature had dropped noticeably. Daniel sneezed again, then coughed. Atena blinked.

"Wait here," she said, and left them standing there, bemused. The children giggled and pointed and whispered but never stopped their preparations.

"Going to be quite a party, sir," Carter said. Unlike Jackson and Teal'C, O'Neill noted, Carter didn't seem to be any more at ease in this place than he was. "Wonder who it's for."

"Probably not us."

"Uh, no." Daniel sneezed again, apologetically. "Sorry." His voice sounded clogged.

As they spoke, Atena returned through one of the doors at the far end of the room, followed by another, younger woman and two men. She nodded to the SG-1 team and made a quick exit, evidently feeling her task was complete and glad of it.

"Who are you?" one of the men said. All three of the newcomers looked tired and impatient and rather apprehensive at the sight of the team.

Of the two men, one had a neatly trimmed gray beard and mustache. He was athletic, but beginning to put on weight. The other, in his late twenties or early thirties, looked as if he would much rather be out playing tennis than swaddled up in rust-colored robes and stuck indoors. He kept glancing around the room, as if checking up on whatever progress the children had made; he was practically dancing on the balls of his feet in his impatience to get away. The woman was midway in age between the two, her features sharp and intent, with dark brown hair beginning to silver at the temples and bright gray eyes.

"We're from Earth," O'Neill said. He was beginning to think he could do this spiel in his sleep by now. "I'm Colonel Jack O'Neill. This is Captain Samantha Carter, Dr. Daniel Jackson, and Teal'C." He watched the three carefully for their reactions, especially to the Jaffa.

None of them seemed especially awed by the man with the golden symbol embossed in his flesh, but they were clearly surprised to see him, recognized the mark, and were respectful and wary of him. They nodded deeply to him, and only as an afterthought to the rest.

"We're looking for the government of this place," Daniel added helpfully.

"Yeah, would that be you?" O'Neill asked, eager to cut to the chase.

"We are the Rejected Ones," the woman said. When the team looked blank, she elaborated, "It is our duty to oversee the comfort of M'kwethet. What do you require?" Her question was addressed to the Jaffa, despite the fact that O'Neill was doing the talking.

"Daniel," O'Neill said, stepping back to make room for the young archaeologist to come forward. "You're on."

Daniel Jackson took a deep breath. "Um, we're looking for the ones who can speak for the whole planet—er, all the people of M'kwethet. We need to warn you of a great danger, to offer you our help and alliance. We come from a place, er, a long way away."

"My name is Alizane Skillkeeper," the woman said. "This"—the older man—"is Jareth of the Manyflowers, and this is Karlanan. If you wish to speak to someone, speak to us. We are the Council of the Rejected Ones of M'kwethet." The look on her face indicated that she really, really hoped they didn't want to speak to anyone at all and if they would just go away it would be a tremendous help. She kept looking at Teal'C, as if waiting for him to take over direction of the discussion.

"And quickly, please," Karlanan snapped, then moderated his tone with an apologetic glance at the Jaffa. "As you can see, my lord, we have much left to do, and very little time. We thought you were the Ones Returning, and we haven't even set up the final selec—"

"Now, now," Jareth chided him. "All will occur in good time. It always has, and always will." He smiled at the team. "I'm sure that our visitors understand why we are preoccupied at the moment, but if necessary—"

The two younger ones exchanged exasperated glances and visibly reined themselves in.

"Do you bring instructions from the Goa'uld?" Alizane demanded. "If so, we are eager to hear them, of course."

Once again picking up his jaw with some difficulty, O'Neill choked out, "Hell, no!"

The Council members exchanged befuddled looks. "But you came through the Gate," Alizane sputtered, as if they had denied it. "Atena told us you came through the Gate."

"We're not from the Goa'uld. We're from another world, called Earth."

The Council communed wordlessly for a moment, with Karlanan glancing frequently over his shoulder, obviously torn between dealing with their visitors and overseeing the hall decorations.

"If you are truly not from the Goa'uld, then we really do not have time to speak to you just now," Jarcth explained at last. "You are welcome to join us at the banquet tonight, of course, and we will be pleased to hear you after the celebration, but this is quite a busy time. Come back this evening, please."

And with that, the Rejected Ones turned on their heels and walked off, their sandals making a rapid patter against the marble floor, leaving SG-1 staring after them dumbfounded.

# CHAPTER THREE

"Oh, dear," O'Neill said, resting the stock of his rifle on the edge of an elaborately carved table. The feet of the table were tree roots, the legs tree trunks; the surface of the tabletop was a mass of low-relief leaves, with birds peeking out here and there. He looked at the table again and shifted his rifle to the floor instead. A little girl, her hands full of flowers, smiled shyly at him until he moved out of her way.

" 'Oh, dear'?" Carter repeated. "Surely you can come up with something better than that. Sir."

"Oh, I don't know, it sort of covers all the bases," Jackson said. "Obviously they've heard of the Goa'uld."

"I have heard of these people, as well," Teal'C said abruptly. "I have not been here before, but I have heard of them."

"Well, spit it out." O'Neill wasn't in the mood for broad hints. "Who are they?"

Teal'C blinked, deciding not to take the remark as a literal invitation, and lifted his massive shoulders in a shrug. "I know only that this is a source of supply for Apophis, and that I was never ordered here. It was never considered a hostile or a dangerous place."

"Which would indicate what? That Apophis didn't see a need for high security here? These people don't look like slaves." Carter gazed at the decorations rapidly being completed around them. "What kind of supplies?"

"All kinds." Teal'C spoke with utter finality.

O'Neill glanced at the big man's midriff, where an infant Goa'uld nestled, and shuddered. "I don't suppose we have to ask you to elaborate on that."

"Maybe we should look around some more," Jackson offered. "Since they seem to be kind of busy."

O'Neill thought about it. "Well, I guess there are worse ways to kill time before the party." The warm, cuddly feeling he'd tried to harbor at first about this world had disappeared entirely. Maybe it was the lack of panic in the eyes of the Rejected Ones—and what kind of name was that for a government, anyway?—when they mentioned the Goa'uld. Of all the people they'd met so far, only the Nox were unconcerned about the Goa'uld. Everybody else was at least wary of them. Why were these people different?

The four team members made their way out of the inner hall and back into the sunshine, somewhat at a loss.

M'kwethet—city, nation, planet?—was clearly gearing up for a major celebration. The preparations in the banquet hall were repeated all over the city. They picked a side street to explore at random, and had to duck and weave among ladders propped against freshly whitewashed walls, and avoid snagging themselves on garlands of flowers looped from window to window.

"This part looks like the Schwarzwald," Carter observed. It was true; away from the central marketplace and the Agora, the architecture had changed. Now, instead of the elegant marble columns, they walked between stuccoed wattle-and-frame houses, with window boxes filled with a riot of flowers overhanging the narrow streets. The streets themselves were cobbled or bare dirt instead of paved with flat slabs of stone, and they rose and fell steeply as they followed the contour of the foothills.

It was as if they had stepped from ancient Greece into medieval Germany, without even a pause for the fall of Rome along the way.

"It's so clean," Jackson murmured, watching with open-mouthed delight as a young man clambered across a steep roof, laying out a complex design in yellow flower petals against the brown thatch. "So pretty." As in many of the oldest Earth cities, the part of the building facing the street was a shop, with each street specializing in its own wares. The one they were walking along at the moment was occupied by weavers, and Carter kept pausing to touch the materials displayed for sale, rubbing them between her fingers as she examined the patterns, colors, and designs.

"Looks nice and peaceful," O'Neill agreed, his voice carefully neutral. He and Carter exchanged knowing glances. Both of them had seen the devastation of Sarajevo, the smoking ruins of Kuwaiti oil fields. Once those places had been "nice and peaceful" too. O'Neill could even remember a time when Beirut, Lebanon, was called the Paris of the East. That was before merely human conflict had overwhelmed that peace. How could M'kwethet maintain "peace" and know about the Goa'uld too?

Whatever the M'kwethet knew about the parasitic aliens, it had nothing to do with conflict. And that was too weird for words, in O'Neill's humble opinion.

"Got any estimates about population, Daniel?" the colonel went on. "Any more ideas on technology?"

"Oh, I don't know." The archaeologist paused for a moment. "I see a lot of very healthy people; that's always a good sign. For population, at least of this city? Anywhere from twenty to fifty thousand. Look up there, in the hills." He pointed. "See the way the houses are built on the hillside? They're surrounded by vineyards and fields. But the roads are dirt or stone. Transportation's still pretty primitive, but it looks like they have aqueducts and irrigation. I haven't seen any steel yet.

"Let's go this way," Jackson went on, picking yet another relatively broad street at right angles to their route, for no particular reason. "Maybe we'll see some more stuff." He led off, his head swiveling back and forth as he tried to see everything they passed. This one featured potters, and they could glimpse shelves upon shelves of ceramic wares, hear the roar of a kiln firing in someone's backyard. A woman was operating a kick wheel, the lump of wet clay transforming like magic into a tall, elegant vase in seconds.

Children played tag, dodging around them, laughing and shouting, using O'Neill as a hiding place. He held still until one of the others ducked around him, and the whole flock ran off again. The colonel followed after Jackson and the others, content to let the scientists gather data for the moment.

The potter cut off the vase and set it on a shelf to dry, letting the wheel spin to stillness as she got up to wash the slurry from her hands.

Down the street, merchants began to close the shutters of their shops, lowering the woven awnings. Bits of cheerful conversation drifted past the team as the work day ended.

There was absolutely nothing threatening in sight.

It just wasn't natural.

"Is it just me, or does anybody else have the beginnings of a bad feeling about this?" O'Neill inquired, elaborately casual.

"I also feel apprehensive," Teal'C rumbled.

"Uh-oh."

"That's what you get for being rhetorical." Carter's hands were tightening about her sidearm. Potter Street was beginning to fall into shadow, and its decorations were almost complete. They passed fewer and fewer people, and all of them seemed to be going the other direction—back to the center of town, to the Gate, to the Agora.

"How long until 'evening'?" Teal'C asked, looking at the sky.

They stopped, indecisive, and the Earth natives instinctively looked at their watches before realizing how irrelevant Earth's chronology was in this alien place. It had been well over two hours since they had stepped through the Stargate.

"Well, it looks like the neighborhood is calling it a day," Jackson observed. "Probably getting ready for the evening meal, or whatever function was being set up in the banquet hall."

"The Agora," O'Neill insisted.

Jackson tilted his head and, after a moment, smiled. "Agora," he conceded.

O'Neill grinned, having won at least one naming issue. "I suppose we could head home for dinner, but I think I feel like eating out tonight. Let's go see what Mom's home cooking is like." He led them back in the direction of the banquet hall.

As they walked they could hear music, erratic and atonal, as if an alien orchestra was tuning up. O'Neill grimaced. Jackson developed that curiously intent look that meant he was deep in the throes of cultural analysis. Carter merely winced and kept on slogging; Teal'C remained, of course, impassive.

More and more people were filling the streets now, all heading in the direction of the M'kwethet Stargate. They pushed past the team, chattering happily; children shrieked and ran, pelting each other with flowers. Young girls stared and pointed at them, giggling behind their hands, and then ran ahead of them. Everyone seemed to have a goal, a place to go and a deadline to meet, and looked extraordinarily happy to be so engaged. It was a celebration, and M'kwethet was well prepared for it.

By the time they came in sight of the central marketplace, the square was packed with people and humming with subdued excitement. A substantial portion of the city population, it seemed, had managed to cram itself either into the square or onto the roofs and balconies of the buildings surrounding it. Carter, being the shortest member of the team, took a cue from several children and climbed up on the stepped base of one of the columns to get a better look.

"They're gathered around the Gate," she reported. "Lined up on either side as if they're waiting—yes! There it goes! The Gate's opening!"

With a hollow whoosh, silvery plasma spurted from the circular Gate. O'Neill glanced around at the natives, expecting expressions of terror, or at least apprehension. Instead he saw eagerness, expectation. All around the Gate platform, what had earlier been a market square was now an assembly area for hundreds of people, watching tensely. The crowd shifted restlessly, and the team wormed their way through, closer to the focus of attention. At the top of the ramp, waiting, were the three Rejected Ones the team had met earlier. They were attired much more formally now. Alizane wore a long red dress, belled out at the knees, with a double apron of a darker red trimmed in white overlapping in front and back. Her sleeves were long and tight, belling at the shoulders. The square bodice was also trimmed in white, and she wore a tall hat that looked like a cone with the tip nipped off, laced once again with white.

The men were dressed in matching red tunics that came to mid-thigh, pinned at each shoulder with a knot of white. Their sandal straps, dyed dark red, wound up their legs to their knees. On their heads they, too, wore the tall hats. It looked as if Karlanan had shaved for the occasion, with a few clumsy nicks in his chin to show for it.

The three of them stood well back from the Gate, out of reach of the billowing plasma, but still on the platform.

As the plasma collapsed back to become the shimmering

surface of the Gate, silence fell over the crowd, as if they were collectively holding their breath.

And then, stepping out of the molten circle, came a humanoid figure. The team's hands clenched their weapons, and Teal'C raised his staff reflexively.

It was not a Serpent Guard.

It was a young man, dressed in a spotless white tunic knotted at the shoulders and a plain gray collar. He was followed by another, similar young man, then a young woman.

As they walked down the ramp, one after another followed them out of the Gate, and the silence broke with screams and cheers. An older woman, her hair streaked with silver, broke out of the crowd and flung herself at one of the newcomers. She was followed almost immediately by others, mothers and fathers and younger siblings by the look of them, welcoming the travelers home. The newcomers came looking for greetings, and they got them. Disregarding all protocol, family members ran up the three steps, grabbing the newcomers as soon as they were recognized. Perhaps a total of a dozen came through the Gate, all young, all unarmed. All, clearly, coming home, to a tumultuous and glad welcome.

And then the crowd at the Gate moved down the steps, and the team watched as the rest of the natives of M'kwethet watched, holding their breath, waiting. Long moments passed, and the cheering died away as the newcomers looked over their shoulders, and the families that greeted them wiped away joyous tears to watch the shimmer of the Gate remain undisturbed.

The Gate shut.

The shimmer disappeared.

An empty circle of stone stood on an empty platform in the middle of the marketplace.

No more young men and women were coming through the Gate.

And somewhere in the crowd, in the silence, a mother wailed in anguish. After a moment she was joined by another, and then a third. The crowd murmured in sympathy and drew away from the wails, migrating instinctively toward joy.

# CHAPTER FOUR

The sound of inconsolable moaning, coming from several locations near the team, raised the hairs on the back of Daniel Jackson's neck. He knew that sound too well—it echoed in his heart and soul every time he remembered his last sight of Sha're. Looking around at the rest of his colleagues, he could tell his friends knew as well as he did what the sound represented. O'Neill's brown eyes were hard, his jaw tight; Carter blinked rapidly at gathering tears. Teal'C seemed unmoved until one glimpsed the shadows in his eyes, the massive fingers tightening around the shaft of the energy lance he carried.

As Daniel watched, the people of M'kwethet began a slow migration up the broad avenue to the portico of the Agora. The farther the newcomers got from the weeping women, the more free they and their families felt to express once more their own joy. Songs broke out as they poured through the columns and into the banquet room.

"It looks like some got away," Carter said, as the team pulled itself together and began to follow the crowd. "I don't understand."

"Or they were sent back." Jackson's voice was raw. " 'Rejected Ones'? Isn't that what Alizane called them?"

"I didn't think the Goa'uld ever let go," O'Neill said thoughtfully. "Apophis seemed pretty happy to kill off anybody he didn't want. Teal'C, what's going on?"

Teal'C shook his head slowly. "I do not know," he answered. "I do not understand this, either."

"Maybe we ought to join the party and see if we can find out."

Despite the light, flippant tone O'Neill used, there was an edge to his words. He was clearly angry, his eyes following the last of the mourners as she stumbled past them, supported by her grieving family. It was Atena, the woman who had first welcomed them to this world. As they watched, she doubled over, hiding her face in her apron as she sobbed. She was surrounded by men and women and children, also weeping, supporting her as she stumbled away from the Gate. The family headed down one of the side streets, and one or two cast resentful glances at the team as they went.

"Well, we were invited." Carter was angry too.

"Yeah." Jackson shoved his glasses up and set his jaw. "Let's go find out."

Inside the newly set-up banquet hall, all restraint caused by the mourning families had been thrown off. A long, narrow table at the end of the room made space for Alizane and her friends, the returning young people and their families. Hardly anyone even looked up at the camouflage-clad Earth team standing in the entryway; they were too busy sharing food and drink and song and laughter. The noise level was just slightly lower than the average rock concert.

Alizane Skillkeeper, however, noticed the newcomers immediately. Passing a golden goblet to Karlanan, who sat beside her, she rose and stepped around one of the Returned Ones, laughing lightly at some remark made to her, and headed directly toward the four. Up close, they could see that the white trim on her dress and hat was made up of dozens of seed pearls.

"Who are you?" she demanded, keeping her voice low and smiling brightly at the nearest partiers as she led them further into the room and off into a corner, near one of the smaller tables. Several of the occupants of the table looked up, offering a pitcher of frothy brown liquid until they saw the grim look in Alizane's eyes. Undaunted, they shrugged and laughed, turning back to their conversation.

"Oh, *now* you want to talk," O'Neill remarked snidely. He was still studying the crowd, especially the individuals who had come through the Gate. Unlike the rest of the M'kwethet citizenry, they were dressed in simple white tunics with gray collars; as he watched, one of them drained a cup and defiantly tore off the collar and threw it to the floor. The others looked stricken at the gesture, until Karlanan roared his approval and urged the rest to do the same. With some urging, they did so, but they were uneasy about it, as if removing the collars was a serious infraction of the rules of polite society.

Alizane ignored the activity at the head table. "Before, you were an annoyance, interrupting our preparations for the Returning. Now you are a problem. The people are beginning to ask questions. Who are you, and where are you from? Why are you using our Gate? Are you from the Goa'uld?" The questions came rapid-fire, without pause. She looked at each of them in turn, expecting answers as a right.

"One thing at a time, please." O'Neill was not inclined to concede her authority just yet. "We told you already, we're not from the Goa'uld. We're from Earth, and we'd like to talk to you, too. For one thing, we'd like to know what you use your Gate for, and how much you know about the Goa'uld."

"Maybe sometime when you're not so busy," Jackson put in, with a meaningful look at his teammates. More and more of the people not immediately involved with the families were paying attention now to the exchange.

O'Neill thought about glaring at the archaeologist, but gave up on the idea. Jackson was incurably civilian. Besides, he seemed distinctly uneasy about something in particular, instead of just feeling spooked about the general ambiance.

And, well, standing around in the middle of a party was possibly not the best place to conduct interstellar negotiations anyway.

O'Neill decided to let it go this time and grill Jackson later.

Alizane, on the other hand, wasn't as willing to drop the subject. She seemed to waver between pursuing the discussion and letting it go. The arrival of Jareth—of the Manyflowers?—appeared to convince her to back off, at least temporarily.

"Be welcome to our Returning, strangers," the older man welcomed them, giving the woman a chiding glance. "Sit with us and share the time of our greatest joy. Eat and drink and sing." He held out an oval metal tray that looked like brass, with engravings outlined in green oxidation. It held four ornately carved wooden mugs filled with the same frothy brown liquid they'd been offered earlier.

The four exchanged glances, and then Jackson reached out to take one of the mugs, lifted it in a toast, and drank. "Thaaaaannnnnnnnk . . ." he gasped, breathing through his mouth.

"Daniel?" Carter asked, worried.

Jackson raised one hand, gasped once or twice, and shook his head. An abrupt flush had colored his fair skin. "Whoa! That has a kick to it." He breathed deeply again. "Really clears the sinuses. Thank you," he went on, addressing an amused Jareth.

"Usually one sips this drink," Jareth advised him with false gravity.

"Now you tell me." Jackson reached for another mug and passed it to O'Neill, pushing it into the colonel's hands. "Try it. Slowly."

O'Neill shook his head. "Nah, I think I'll be the designated driver this trip. Carter, you try. A little sip."

Carter, torn between resentment at being the designated guinea pig and interest in the strange brew, accepted and sipped gingerly. Her reaction, while not as pronounced as Jackson's, indicated general approval. "Not bad, sir."

"Join us," Jareth repeated. "Please. The discussions we need to have can wait until after the celebration, as we first planned."

"The matter is important," Alizane snapped. "We need to know who these people are."

"You were willing to wait until you got the party decorations up," Carter pointed out. She put the cup on a nearby table, freeing her hands. "A little while longer shouldn't make any difference. Unless you're expecting more guests."

The other woman gave her a poisonous glare. "I have asked the Returned Ones, and they know nothing of you. You are strangers. We need to know why you're using our Gate."

Jareth smiled, set down the tray, and slipped an arm around Alizane's shoulders. "Come, Skillkeeper. It's the time to rejoice at the addition to our numbers, not to challenge peaceful visitors." He pointedly did not glance at the hands hovering near sidearms. "This is a joyous time. Grief will come later, as it always does. Leave it until later." He led the woman away, casting an apologetic look over his shoulder at O'Neill. The colonel shook his head. He didn't envy the other man the task of sharing power, or whatever it was, with an unpredictable, bubbling volcano.

Once the two had returned to the head table, Carter glanced at O'Neill for permission. When he nodded, both Carter and Jackson moved out into the banquet room, eventually joining a group of beribboned young people at a lower table. Carter seated herself between two blond young men and began a banter that could almost be called flirting; Jackson was asking a young lady for an explanation of the design on a cup.

O'Neill accepted a small loaf of brown bread from a passing servitor and chewed thoughtfully, watching his two teammates talking and laughing and drinking, while Teal'C frowned and remained stubbornly on guard. "Ah, to be young again," the colonel remarked ironically. "I used to be able to stay up and party all night like that, how about you?"

"No," the other man demurred. "Jaffa do not party."

"What a surprise." O'Neill shook his head. "Do you have any idea why Daniel would have decided to postpone a perfectly good discussion?"

"Perhaps he felt that it was a public place, and if the conversation had continued that Alizane Skillkeeper would create a scene which would not be conducive to progress in negotiations."

O'Neill raised an eyebrow. "You think?"

Teal'C raised a brow back, and O'Neill smiled a little.

Then he shook his head. "Something's still seriously bugging me about this place—I feel like I left the water running or something. I think I'm going to do a little prowling around, see what I can see. Stay here and keep an eye on the kids, will you?"

"Captain Carter is a competent warrior," Teal'C observed.

"Yeah, well, just in case. And I notice you don't say much about Daniel. He needs you."

Teal'C nodded and took up a position of parade rest, as inconspicuous as a tiger at the party. He ignored the surreptitious glances coming from several of the tables and maintained a steady scan of the entire room, from the head table at one end to the rows of connected tables filled with what appeared to be ordinary citizens at the other end of the room.

Meanwhile, Samantha Carter was enjoying herself. It

wasn't often that she felt she could let her guard down on a new world, but sitting at this table felt like the good old days back in the dormitory. The twins sitting across from her looked at her with the same awe she used to get from freshmen when she was a senior counselor.

"Is it true you're from another world?" Dane asked, filling her cup again. She nodded thanks and drank deeply. The stuff didn't really have *that* much of a kick.

"Yes," she answered. "We're from Earth."

"What's Earth like?" Dane's brother, Markhtin, wanted to know.

Sitting next to him, Daniel gave her a crooked little smile, letting her know she was on her own for this one.

"Well," she temporized, "it's beautiful. A lot like your world. Blue skies, green trees. We haven't been here very long, you know, so it's hard to make comparisons."

"Do you serve the Goa'uld on Earth?"

Markhtin gave him a scornful glance. "Of course they do."

"No, we don't," Daniel contradicted firmly. "We're free. And we're fighting the Goa'uld."

The twins, and several of their companions who had eavesdropped on the conversation, looked blank, as if unable to process this idea.

"It's true," Carter said. "We fight the Goa'uld."

"But *why*?" a girl sitting farther down the table wanted to know.

The two team members from Earth blinked. "Because we want to *stay* free," Carter said at last, taking a piece of fruit from the tray between them. After a moment she realized she had absolutely no idea how one went about eating it. Dane smiled apologetically, taking it from her and peeling away the fuzzy outer skin to reveal large, meaty golden seeds. He popped one out to place in his mouth before handing the fruit back to her.

"Thanks," she said, prying one of the seeds loose. The

skin burst in her mouth, releasing a tart juice and sweetish pulp. "Hey, this is really good."

"It's my favorite," Markhtin said with a proprietary smile. "Do you have anything like that on your Earth?"

"Pomegranates," Daniel supplied, watching Carter's expression. "Only pomegranate seeds are red, not yellow."

Markhtin looked put out that his favorite wasn't as unique as he thought. Daniel hastened to change the subject yet again. "So this party is to celebrate your people coming back from the Goa'uld. How long does the celebration continue?"

"Oh, it started days ago, with the last contests," Dane said. "And it will go on until the Chosen are sent out."

"*We're* the winners," Markhtin announced. At a glare from one of the others at the table, he added, "Everybody here, I mean." He looked at the SG-1 members. "Except you, of course."

"What do you contest for?"

Carter looked up sharply at the tone of Daniel's voice. He was asking the question as if he already knew the answer.

"To be Candidates for the next Choosing," Markhtin replied proudly. "That's us."

"And you're chosen for . . . ?"

"The next group to go to the Goa'uld, to the honor of M'kwethet and our ancient agreement." The last phrase was recited as if by rote.

Carter and Daniel exchanged looks and simultaneously reached for their cups. This was going to take some more discussion.

"You know," Daniel said carefully, "there are reasons you might not want to do that."

"It's the highest honor we have!" someone down the table said indignantly.

In the shadows, Teal'C stirred, then subsided again.

* * *

O'Neill took his time walking back down to the square,
paying attention to the shadows and the glow of moonlight
on white stone, trying to figure out why his feeling of
unease was growing with every step. It wasn't as if he was
being followed—he was all too familiar with that particular sensation. And it wasn't even, exactly, the bizarre
attitude the inhabitants of this world seemed to have about
the Goa'uld. There was something else.

Something wrong.

Something missing.

Something.

The awnings over the small shops had been pulled
down. The little windows and low doors were black holes
that he stared into, trying to analyze the feeling. It wasn't
as if something was watching him—not even the stray dog
sniffing through the garbage twenty feet away was paying
him any attention. Several times he stopped, staring at the
walls, the stars, the cobblestones, his frustration growing.
It made no sense, none at all; if there was something seriously out of synch on this world, it was Daniel Jackson's
job to notice it, and Daniel hadn't said anything. Except, of
course, interrupting his discussion with Alizane, but whatever was bugging him had nothing to do with the Council
members. It was something else. He just couldn't put his
finger on it, and he *ought* to be able to. . . .

The marketplace was deserted at this hour, filled only
with shadows. The Gate loomed over it, a brooding stone
circle standing atop the three-step platform; a pair of
moons provided barely enough light for the rim to cast
a shadow. O'Neill stood in the middle of the circle of
shadow and turned in place, surveying the square yet again
in the different perspective of darkness. A few lights
showed through windows, but all the noise and life of the
city was up the hill, at the Agora. The Gate might have

been nothing more than an oddly shaped monument, standing in lonely glory on top of the platform.

His fingertips tapped nervously on the butt of his pistol, making a soft brushing sound. It wasn't even as if it was too quiet; the dog was snuffling, a cluster of insects buzzed from one bit of debris to another, a bird chirped sleepily to itself.

He turned again.

Gate.

Buildings, streets, decorations. Everything was exactly the same as it was when they'd arrived, only a few hours before. Maybe it was just the unusual circumstance of arriving in the middle of a busy town. After all, how often had the Goa'uld put Gates and all their associated technology right in the middle . . . ?

Associated technology.

O'Neill spun, searching, a cold chill wrapping its fingers around his gut. Gate. Platform. Buildings. Shops. Everything normal, everything where it should be, except—

Where was the Dial-Home Device?

# CHAPTER FIVE

In the darkness, O'Neill swept from one end of the square to the other, his search thorough, efficient, studying every wall, every pile of garbage, even the stones paving the streets to see if somehow they formed the symbols the Gate system used. The team carried with them a signal device that would open the iris barrier at the Earth Gate, but they had always depended on finding a DHD on the other end to operate the Gate for their return home. The DHD, the Dial-Home Device, was the control panel, the giant keyboard that encoded the Gate symbols. Normally it was quite close to the Gate itself, usually taking the form of a large flat dome of concentric circles, with the series of alien symbols matching the ones on the Gate set on push-plates. Pressing the symbols programmed the Gate to open the wormhole home. Gates opened in only one direction; you couldn't open one, go through, and then turn around and go back. So there was always a DHD with the Gate—always.

Not this time.

There was nothing like a DHD anywhere in sight.

He quelled a cold surge of panic. It had to be here somewhere. It had to. If it wasn't, he and his team were going to be stuck here, on a world that couldn't possibly have the technology to build a new operating console. They'd be at the mercy of whoever was on the other end, and from the sound of Alizane's questions, the other end meant Goa'uld.

Maybe Hammond would send a team after them to find out what happened—but that would just mean another Stargate team trapped forever.

"Exactly what did you think you were doing, Colonel?" He could practically hear Hammond erupting all over him, and couldn't blame him. The first thing, always the first thing to do when entering enemy territory was to secure the line of retreat. He'd been so busy gawking at being gawked at, he hadn't even bothered to look, didn't even notice that the DHD wasn't there. He'd led his people away and let the Gate shut behind them exactly like a trapdoor.

He could see himself answering, too. "Well, sir, there was this garden path we went wandering down . . ."

No. No time for jokes now. He stopped, forced himself to take a deep breath, then another. Good thing the others weren't around to see him running around like a beheaded chicken. All right, so he couldn't find the damned thing. That didn't mean it wasn't here. The natives, or at least the Rejected Ones, would certainly know where it was. They were accustomed to the Gate being used, so certainly they must know how to do it themselves. Daniel and Teal'C might not think that talking to Alizane in public was a great idea, but right now he was going to reconsider that idea.

Or not. *Don't overreact*, he told himself. There wasn't any point in letting the whole planet know that the four of them were isolated and alone with no way home. First consult with the rest of the team.

Taking another deep breath, he squared his shoulders and started back toward the lights and music and laughter coming from the Agora crowning the distant hill. Time to share the bad news and figure out what to do next.

"Garden path?" Teal'C interposed, confused. "I did not see a garden."

O'Neill opened his mouth to explain and then shrugged. Teal'C frowned a little more deeply. It was one of those mysterious cultural things, then. He would demand an explanation later. Though it would never do to let O'Neill know, he rather enjoyed putting the colonel to the trouble. It never failed to exasperate the other man. It never stopped Teal'C from baiting him, either.

Jackson, who got the reference, was also frowning, and as always his expression failed to disguise his inner feelings. "Jack?"

O'Neill took a deep breath, thinking as he did so that if he kept it up, he'd end up hyperventilating for sure. "Er, yes. In a manner of speaking."

He'd pulled the other members of the team out of the banquet hall with some difficulty. Both Jackson and Carter were reluctant to leave their new friends, and were already beginning to show signs of having overindulged in that brown drink. Their companions at the table were reluctant to let them go, but a glare from Teal'C made them subside, however reluctantly.

Once outside, Carter and Jackson were sufficiently sober and sufficiently professional to register shock and alarm at the idea of the missing DHD, however. Now, standing together some distance from the colonnaded portico of the Agora, they put their heads together.

"It's got to be there shomewhere," Carter slurred, then corrected herself through sheer force of will. "Somewhere. Doesn't it? Teal'C?"

"I have never visited a world which did not have one," the big man admitted. "Presumably the one here is hidden somewhere, perhaps to prevent inadvertent activation."

O'Neill considered the possibility that a kid could open a Gate while playing, and shuddered. "Okay. I'll buy that. But it does mean that we're stuck here until we find it. I don't plan to camp out in the village square, and I don't think I want to ask our hosts for the address of the nearest motel just yet. So come on, folks, we're going for a little hike out of town."

Carter shook her head. "Waitaminit, shir—sir. We need to finish some ver'—very important confersations back at the party."

O'Neill stared at her incredulously. "Just what the hell is *in* that brown stuff, Captain? I gave you an order."

Jackson raised a placating hand. "No, wait, she'sh right. If we just *go*"—he swung around in an erratic circle, arm outstretched, presumably indicating whatever direction they might take—"well, that's shushpitious. The kids might follow us. Besides, we were in the middle of this *really* intereshting convershation. 'Bout Goa'uld. And stuff."

Carter nodded dumbly, her eyes huge and pleading.

O'Neill turned on Teal'C. "I thought I asked you to keep an eye on these two."

Teal'C's expression remained bland. "I observed them very carefully at all times. They did not appear to be in danger."

"Incapacitated is not danger?" O'Neill threw up his hands in disgust. "I hate this world. I want that in the record: I hate this world. Go on back, then. But *no more liquor*. That's a direct order, you hear me? And I expect you back out here in . . ." He grabbed a number out of the air. "Twenty minutes. Otherwise we're going to come in after you, and I promise you it won't be pretty. Understand?"

Carter saluted, in a wobbly fashion. Jackson jerked his head up and down and nearly fell over. The two of them supported each other up the steps, and O'Neill glared at the fourth member of the team.

"Some baby-sitter *you* are," he snarled.

"People on your world sit on babies?"

"I don't suppose we could claim there was some mysterious alien influence on the two of you?" O'Neill asked the next morning, surveying the ruins of the two scientists before him. When Carter and Jackson had left the banquet the second time, their friends had followed, waving fond farewells, but had made no effort to follow them away from the Agora. After a good hour's walk, the team had made their way out of the city, climbing up into the low hills surrounding it. They finally made camp by a small waterfall on a bluff that overlooked the city but was remote from the houses that terraced the hills.

O'Neill and Teal'C had awakened with the sunrise, made a small fire and heated field rations. Jackson and Carter had tried to ignore the whole concept of morning, moaning and hiding their heads. Apparently the brown drink had a particularly nasty afterlife. "Or are you both just cheap dates?"

Jackson flinched and made a pleading gesture, probably related to the volume of O'Neill's voice. Carter, who knew that the deceptively pleasant voice of her commanding officer wasn't any louder than usual, surreptitiously dry-swallowed aspirin from her field pack instead.

"Share, Captain," O'Neill ordered gently. Her attempt hadn't been surreptitious enough. She took a deep, careful breath and handed the bottle to her fellow hangover victim. The plastic top clattered on the rocks at their feet, and they winced simultaneously. "I'll take that as a 'no' for the alien influence theory.

"On the one hand," their team commander went on, still in a conversational tone, "I don't think Hammond would consider a hangover an adequate excuse for failure to report for duty. I think I'd have to agree with him.

"On the other hand, my team is clearly not up to snuff."

He sounded regretful. Carter gave him an apprehensive, bloodshot glance.

"There's always the possibility that M'kwethet holds the secret of the ultimate cure for the morning after, though."

"That would be worthwhile," Jackson mumbled. "Definitely worthwhile." He fumbled with the bottle, struggling to replace the snap-on cap.

"Then there's the offensive capability of M'kwethet booze," O'Neill went on. "I see a lot of casualties here. Fifty percent. Impressive."

Carter glared.

"However, all that is absolutely irrelevant, because if we're ever going to get home again we'd better all shape up and fly right. I invite you to go duck your heads under that waterfall and see if that will help. I *think* the water's above freezing . . ."

Some time later, the team gathered in a rough circle, seating themselves on rocks tumbled off the side of the hill. Jackson's wet hair stood up in spikes. He looked slightly better than he had half an hour before. Carter had improved, too, though perhaps not quite as much. She looked as if the whole experience had been filed away in the back of her mind as Let's Not Try That Stuff Again Ever.

"Okay, people, let's recap," O'Neill said briskly, as if drafting a mission report. "We arrived on NPR seven six three zero niner to find the inhabitants preparing for a celebration and were invited to participate. Our esteemed scientific staff felt that full participation would assist in gaining the inhabitants' confidence."

"Hmph," chorused the esteemed scientific staff, clutching their heads.

"The natives, who call the world M'kwethet, were celebrating the arrival of a bunch of kids through the Stargate," O'Neill went on.

"We were unable to ascertain their point of origin," Teal'C put in.

O'Neill nodded. "But based on the way they were welcomed, it looked like they were coming home."

"Home from where?" Jackson challenged blurrily. Not even a hangover could keep a good scientist down. At least his enunciation was improving.

"Unknown at this time." O'Neill took a deep breath. "It also looked like not everybody made it back, based on the reaction of some of the natives."

For a moment there was silence, as the team exchanged somber glances. Each of them had experienced the joy of coming home even as they knew some of their own comrades would never know that joy again. "Coming home" was an experience that would always be alloyed with a guilty sorrow.

"Could they have escaped from the Goa'uld?" Carter wanted to know.

"No," Teal'C said definitely.

O'Neill waited politely for the Jaffa to continue. When the silence stretched out and it was plain that Teal'C was not going to explain, the colonel confirmed his response. "No. They didn't show any apprehension about being pursued. They didn't look scared. They were . . . coming home." He took a deep breath. "The mission has been complicated by the fact that so far we have failed—I have failed—to locate the Dial-Home Device. Without that, we're screwed.

"All of this tells me that we'd better get our asses back to town and get our job done right this time. There's something funny going on there and I'd like to know what it is. At the same time, we must locate that DHD."

Jackson took one last swallow of water from his canteen. "Yeah," he said, his voice marginally clearer. "That would be a good idea."

"We also need to find out where those kids came from," O'Neill went on, "and what they were doing there." *And what about the ones who didn't come back?* he added silently. "I suggest you eat something. You're going to need your strength. I want to move out no later than ten hundred hours. We're wasting daylight up here."

Carter closed her eyes, her face a study in misery. "Yes, sir," she whispered.

"And I expect you to be combat-ready."

"Yes, sir." If it weren't for the sibilants, no one could have heard her.

"Monster," Jackson added. But he was already reviving at the prospect of returning to a new culture. Not being military, he could get away with such remarks.

O'Neill chose to take it as a compliment anyway. "Ten hundred hours," he repeated. "Be there or be square."

"How does one become square?" Teal'C inquired.

O'Neill opened his mouth, closed it again, and shrugged.

Carter and Jackson crawled away.

Apparently Carter and Jackson were not the only ones suffering from the aftereffects of the party. As the team came back into M'kwethet, they saw a market square that resembled Times Square on January 1—with the Sanitation Department on holiday. There weren't any plastic cups, beer cans, or silly hats, but there was debris, the occasional slime-sign where someone hadn't held his liquor, and the ribbons that had spiraled up the Grecian columns hung in tatters.

A goat nibbled on the former contents of an overturned cart.

A little girl sat on the edge of a well at one side of the square, thumb firmly in her mouth, and stared up at them without apparent surprise.

"Hi," Jackson said.

"Hi," the little girl responded, without removing her thumb.

"Didn't your mother ever tell you not to talk to strangers?" O'Neill asked rhetorically.

"No." Apparently this world had adopted Greek architecture but ignored rhetoric.

"They aren't afraid of what comes through the Gate,"

Carter observed. There was still a furrow of residual pain between her blond brows, but it hadn't affected her powers of observation. "Maybe the Goa'uld don't come here."

"No." Teal'C was puzzled. "They do. I have seen shipments of goods and slaves I was told were from this world. This is a safe supply world for Apophis. And the Councilors know of them."

"Then the DHD has got to be here somewhere," O'Neill concluded. "It's not as if somebody can open up a wormhole from the other end and pull them through the wrong way. But *where*?"

Sharing an expression of bewilderment, they started down the cobbled street, heading back to the Agora for lack of a better destination. The little girl, still sucking her thumb, watched them go.

The banquet hall wasn't in much better shape than the square; the only difference was that a handful of people were making a desultory effort to clean up. Overseeing the effort, the team saw with varying levels of surprise, was Jareth of the Manyflowers. A look of resignation crossed the man's face as he caught sight of them. Apparently Jareth had been the M'kwethet designated driver; he showed no ill effects from last night's party. His beard was neatly combed, his hair in a neat series of curls across his forehead, bound back by a white band. He was wearing a red open coat over a spotless white short tunic this morning, and the straps of his sandals looked new.

"Excuse us," O'Neill said. It was a little unnerving to see so little reaction to their presence. Usually, when they met autochtons (Daniel liked that term better than "natives," possibly because he was the only one who could pronounce it), they were regarded with either awe or patronizing pleasantry. But they had never before been treated as a mere nuisance. "You said yesterday that you'd meet with us after the banquet. We weren't able to talk then. But we'd like to do so now."

Jareth looked annoyed. "You left. This, however, is still not a good time. We are quite busy, as you can see. There is much work left to be done here, and not much time to do it in."

"Yes, I can see that."

The cleaning staff made an effort to move a little faster under the sharp scowl of their supervisor.

"I can see that," O'Neill repeated, as Jareth turned away to give directions to new additions to the cleaning staff. He let his impatience show. "Look, we've come a long way and we've got some really important stuff to talk about. If you're not the man, then can you direct us to someone who is?"

" 'The man'?" Jareth inquired, confused. As he tried to follow the colloquialism, he looked up to greet Karlanan, who, coming from one of the rooms at the rear of the building, obviously had not been designated to drive anyone anywhere. Unlike the older Jareth, Karlanan still showed the effects of the night's endeavors: red eyes, stained clothing, uncombed hair. He had the air of a man who was up too early and very much against his will. O'Neill was sure that members of his own team felt a certain empathy.

The younger Council member was carrying a large shallow glazed pot, yellow with black figures etched in the fired surface. He bore it with considerable care, as if afraid he might drop it. Jackson stepped forward as though to examine the object more closely, and the other man frowned and shifted it away, protecting it with his body. Meanwhile, Jareth looked relieved, as if he'd been waiting for this for some time, and its arrival was a welcome distraction. "Good," he said, addressing Karlanan and turning away from SG-1. "Have the lots been distributed?"

Karlanan nodded and winced, as if he regretted moving his head. "Alizane defined the tribute this morning. You want the bowl on the altar?"

"Naturally." Jareth's attention was back on the cleanup crew and the arrangements before him.

Trying desperately to retrieve the conversation, Daniel Jackson said, "Uh, what the colonel means is—"

"I think he knows perfectly well what we mean," O'Neill snapped. He was heartily tired of the diplomatic approach by this time. "Trust me, Jareth, we're not going to go away without some answers. We want to talk to the governing body of this world. That seems to be you. We know you know about the Goa'uld, so presumably you know about the threat they pose. We want to see if we can help each other. We also need information about your Gate controls."

Across the room, someone dropped a plate. All work stopped as the cleanup crew stared at the man who had raised his voice to their Councilors.

The Earth team's eruption made a flustered Jareth escort all of them, Karlanan included, to a room behind the main hall, leaving the cleanup crew with only hasty instructions. The mention of the Goa'uld and of the Gate in the same sentence, or perhaps the forcefulness of O'Neill's delivery, seemed to have finally gotten his attention. Karlanan put his precious pot on a small table in the back of the room and ran for Alizane, doubtless to provide moral leadership to the Council of the Rejected Ones.

"We're from Earth," O'Neill explained once more, with very little patience, once Alizane had arrived. "We came through the Gate. Doesn't that mean anything to you?"

The three looked at each other with obvious confusion.

"What is Earth?" Alizane asked.

"It's a world far away," Carter answered, forestalling yet another explosion on O'Neill's part. "We have a Gate, too. We used the Gate to come here. We've been to many worlds. We're traveling to all the different places we can, looking for allies against the Goa'uld."

The Council of the Rejected Ones looked at each other, still bewildered.

"I know it's a lot to take in all at once," Daniel said. "But it's important. We saw some of your people come through the Gate yesterday. Where did they go? Where did they come from?"

"And how did they get there in the first place?" O'Neill snapped.

Karlanan shook his head like a man missing something important. "They came back. They are the Rejected Ones."

"I thought you were the Rejected Ones," O'Neill snapped.

"We are." The Council looked at each other in helpless confusion.

Daniel drew in a sharp breath, as if a light had gone on. "Who rejected you?"

"The Goa'uld, of course." Alizane shook her head. "Are you not also Rejected Ones? How else could you come here?"

O'Neill opened his mouth as if to make a snide remark, then thought better of it. "The Goa'uld are our enemies. They're your enemies, too."

Jareth was still confused. "The Goa'uld pose no threat to us."

The team looked at each other incredulously. "They don't?"

"No. Of course not." All three of the M'kwethet looked as if Jareth had stated the blindingly obvious. "They are not our enemies. We do not wish to be enemies to the Goa'uld."

SG-1 was baffled. "Excuse us," Daniel said politely, "I'd like to consult my colleagues for a moment."

He herded them across the room, muttering, "Time out for a huddle, guys." Glancing over at the puzzled M'kwethet, he went on, "I think they're serious."

O'Neill shook his head. "I don't get it."

"I think we're wasting our time," Carter said. "They obviously don't perceive the Goa'uld as a threat. They're not going to be interested in helping us."

"Agreed," rumbled Teal'C.

"Okay, fine. They don't want to help us. Let's buckle down and find that control and get the hell out of here. Any world that knows the Goa'uld and doesn't think they're a threat isn't going to be any help to us."

"No," Jackson interrupted, craning his neck to get a good view of the pot on the table. "I think we ought to stay."

Now it was O'Neill's turn to look exasperated. "You always do that. Why do you always do that? Why should we stay this time?" A part of him was ironically pleased at the presumption that *of course* they were going to be able to leave—that they even had a choice of whether to stay or not.

"I'd like to know more about these people," Jackson said, still peering around Karlanan. "You mentioned lots? Tribute?" The questions were directed to Jareth.

Jareth evidently felt that someone on the Earth team was finally showing signs of intelligence. "Yes, of course."

"When do you draw lots?"

"Tomorrow afternoon. The tribute will be sent in only three days. So you can understand why we are so busy just now."

"Oh, definitely. Of course." Jackson was nodding as if he agreed, but there was something in his eyes that made O'Neill suspicious. The colonel was beginning to see where the questions were going, and he didn't like it. At all. "How many?"

Jareth looked at Karlanan, who took a deep breath before answering. "Alizane said there would be twenty this time."

"Twenty?" Jackson echoed Jareth, but with more horror.

O'Neill held his temper with effort. "What the hell are you talking about?" he said, hoping he was wrong.

"Twenty," Karlanan confirmed. "Ten of the young women, ten of the young men will go to the Goa'uld in tribute this season."

# CHAPTER SIX

"Are you *serious*?" O'Neill roared.

"It has precedent, in fact. The legend of the Minotaur, Theseus and the Labyrinth. Sending the tribute to Crete." Jackson was still horrified, but fascinated as well. "These people seem to have—have actually reached an accommodation with the Goa'uld."

"It is not impossible," Teal'C confirmed. "So long as they send their best, it would be reasonable for the Goa'uld to accept it. It would be easier than expending resources to force the same result. And it would account for this world as a supply depot."

"And we do send our best," Jareth assured them, as Alizane and Karlanan nodded earnest agreement. "We select our very best young people. They have known for months who may be selected—they compete for the honor of being Chosen. Tomorrow we draw lots for the necessary number, and two days after that the Gate will open for them. The Goa'uld have been satisfied with this arrangement for generations."

O'Neill stepped forward, moving Jackson aside. "I'll bet they have! Are you telling us you deliberately send—"

"That confirms what we were told last night," Carter muttered, casting an uneasy glance at her enraged commander. "Sir, it's a deeply ingrained part of their culture."

O'Neill wheeled on her. " 'Ingrained'?" What the hell are you talking about? In case you've forgotten, Captain, we're not operating under some damned Prime Directive here! These people are sacrificing their children!"

Carter blinked. The subject of children was a particularly sensitive one with the colonel. And she wasn't entirely indifferent to it herself. In light of what she'd just heard, a lot of last night's conversation, about Choosing, the intense fascination with what lay on the other side of the Gate, suddenly made more sense. At least, what she could remember of it did.

"It is an honorable sacrifice," Alizane interrupted sharply. "We keep our world safe—"

"Sure, you send out your young people so you can be safe—"

"We are the Rejected Ones! We know exactly what they are sent to. We have *been* where they go." Alizane stared directly up into O'Neill's eyes from a distance of less than arm's length. "Who are you to tell us what we should do?"

"We're the people who have the guts to fight the Goa'uld!"

"Sir—" Carter tried desperately to interrupt as more and more of the previous evening's conversation came back to her.

"You are warriors, then? You go and fight. Tell me, does no one die in your battles?"

"Yes, some of us are warriors. And people die in battle . . ."

"How many have you lost?" Alizane interrupted. "More, I think, than we have! Our way is better. We cannot fight the Goa'uld. No one can." Behind her, Jareth and Karlanan nodded in confirmation.

"These people can," Teal'C interrupted. "I have seen it. I have joined them because of it."

Alizane gave him an incredulous look. "You are Jaffa. You of all people know better."

"I am Jaffa, and I know what I know."

"I know you are wrong."

"And I know you're nuts," O'Neill snarled, turning to go.

The rest of the team prepared to follow.

"We go willingly and joyously!" Alizane's voice was rising defensively. "Come to the drawing of the lots and see!"

" 'Willingly and joyously,' my ass." O'Neill was practically frothing as they descended the steps of the banquet hall. "I've been through an induction lottery, too, and there's nothing joyous about it, dammit."

"Colonel, wait." Carter reached out and grabbed O'Neill's arm, stopping him in the middle of the square. "We can't just walk out and let them get away with this."

"I don't see how we can stop it," Jackson muttered.

"I do," Carter responded, "but we're going to have to stay a while longer."

O'Neill slammed to a halt, causing the rest of the team—except for Teal'C—to collide with each other like railroad cars. "Speak to me, Captain."

"Some of the things the kids told me last night make sense to me now." The blond captain bit her lip. "I don't think some of those kids are as enthusiastic about this stuff as the Council says they are. I don't think they really understand what they're heading into. They wanted to talk about it some more, then Alizane came by and they clammed up. But a couple of them asked me to come talk to them today. I, um, I promised I would. I think I should."

"I agree," Teal'C said. "If they truly realized what awaits them they would not be so quick to volunteer."

"Well, the thing is, if the ones who come back are Rejected Ones, that means that Alizane and the rest do know." Daniel was trying hard to remain logical and dispassionate. "And they send the kids anyway. How can they do that?"

"They have decided on an acceptable level of casualties." The Jaffa was, as usual, impassive. "Clearly they do not inform the new Candidates. As soon as the Rejected Ones return, they must be brought into a conspiracy of silence so that the young people will continue to view selection as a great honor."

"Acceptable!" Carter erupted. "Colonel, what if some of those kids don't want to go? They sure wouldn't if they had all the facts. Shouldn't they have the chance?"

O'Neill stared at her for a long moment before murmuring, "It's a long way to Canada, Carter."

"Sir?" For a moment Carter had completely lost track of her commanding officer's train of thought.

"Never mind, Captain." O'Neill sighed. "All right. If you've got a meeting already set up with some of these kids, go for it. Daniel, let's do a little recon and see if we can find the DHD in daylight. Teal'C, you go with Carter. Maybe you can convince them." The colonel gave a queasy look at the Jaffa's midsection. Teal'C nodded in grim acknowledgement.

It was impossible for Carter, clad in camouflage fatigues, and Teal'C, carrying a Goa'uld energy weapon and marked with the sign of Apophis, to move through the town unremarked. Therefore, they made no attempt to be furtive. Teal'C strode down the cobbled streets like a massive ship plowing through familiar seas, and Carter scurried in his wake. The inhabitants of M'kwethet saw him coming and made it a point to get out of his way. When the black man came to a stop at an intersection she nearly ran into him.

"What is the location of the meeting you spoke of?" Teal'C demanded.

"I was wondering when you were going to ask that," Carter snipped. "If you'd slow down a little I could lead the way."

Teal'C frowned down at her feet. "Your legs are too short."

"My what?"

"Lead."

Carter continued to splutter, but more suspiciously now. "You're teasing me, aren't you? You've been hanging out with O'Neill too long."

Teal'C merely stood at parade rest, patiently waiting.

"Oh, for crying out loud," she muttered, unconsciously mimicking the colonel herself, and looked around to get her bearings.

It was difficult to remember through the alcoholic haze of the night before, but surely Markhtin and Dane had said something about the Street of the Bakers, and there was an appetizing thread of an aroma coming from the west. Looking past the banners of welcome, she could see a blue sign hanging from an awning, a picture of an ear of wheat and a brown lump that probably stood for bread. Several other signs hanging from other shopfronts echoed the same theme.

"There," she said with more confidence than she felt. "That's the place."

"You are sure?"

Carter merely glared at him and marched off in the direction of the sign. After a moment, Teal'C followed. The astute observer might have seen the slightest twitch in the corner of his mouth.

The shop, or house, or both, appeared to be closed for the day. The door, brown wooden planks crossed with blue supports, remained firmly shut. The ubiquitous awning, this one striped a cheerful green and white, remained down, reaching from the roofline of the first floor three-quarters of the way to the ground. The only window they could see, on the other side of the door, was small and nearly opaque, with thick yellow glass.

The Jaffa stood by patiently. Impassively.

Carter made a face and a fist and pounded on the door.

The window swung two inches out from the wall and back again.

Moments later the door opened, and a blond man in his late teens stared at them, wide-eyed.

"Dane?" Carter asked uncertainly.

An identical blond man popped up beside the first, blinked at the sight of the alien visitors, and hurriedly waved them into the house, smiling broadly.

"Sam Carter," the second twin said, leading them deeper into the house. "We are pleased you came. You said you would tell us more about your world beyond the Gate."

The front of the house was obviously used as the bakery shop; a wide counter covered with flour dust showed where bread had been kneaded, and several thick brown ceramic bowls were covered with damp cloths, indicating dough was still rising. Light came from the small window and from two oil lamps placed strategically in front of reflectors; when the awning was up, the room would be open and bright. Shelves behind the main counter held the remnants of the previous day's work, in long, complicated twisted loaves and smaller, rounder lumps that resembled the image on the sign outside. No ovens were visible; Carter guessed they must be behind the house, lessening the danger from fire. The whole house smelled of yeast and fresh-baked bread, making Carter's mouth water.

The hallway that led from shop to living quarters was dark and small. She glanced behind her to see Teal'C filling up the passageway, blocking whatever light was available from the lamps. She was relieved to find them entering a larger room with a massive table and a huge open combination cabinet and sideboard; it was clearly the central eating and gathering place for the family. Judging from the size of the table, there were many more family members or apprentices around than were immediately visible. Carter wondered where everyone else was. Back at the Agora, perhaps, still celebrating?

"We're eager to hear more about your world, too," Carter said as she and the twins seated themselves around the table. The chairs were equally massive and, like most of the furniture she'd seen on this world, intricately carved. She scooted forward; the high relief made the back of the chair uncomfortable to lean against, however lovely the tree motif might be. The table itself was empty, its wood, like that of all the furniture, polished to a high golden gleam.

Teal'C remained standing, on guard, next to the door.

"Uh, where's your family? And what about the rest of your friends?" Carter went on.

The twins shared an identical blink. "Our father and sisters are at the Great Hall, of course. It's the celebration time. Some of the servants are in the back, tending the ovens, but they'll join them as soon as they're finished. Our friends"—they smiled—"well, we wanted to speak to you first. We can invite them later." The two of them spoke together, alternating sentences. It made it even more difficult to keep track of which one was which. Carter was grateful they were sitting next to one another; it was like following a tennis match.

"Is it true that you've been to other worlds?" one twin—probably Dane—asked.

"Yes," Carter nodded. "Many worlds. Through the Gate."

"And you have seen the Goa'uld?" Markhtin wanted to know.

"Yes." Carter glanced over her shoulder to the Jaffa.

"Is he a Goa'uld?" The twins were alternating questions now, rapid-fire.

"No!" Teal'C rumbled.

"You serve them, then. You have the Sign that the Rejected Ones describe. Is it true that they live in palaces made of gold?"

"And ivory?"

"Does it hurt to have that thing put on your forehead?"

"And are there thousands of people?"

"Jareth tells stories of great magic. Are they true?"

"Really?"

Obviously this last point was one about which they felt considerable skepticism.

"Wait, wait." Carter raised her hand. "One thing at a time, okay? First, we've never been to the Goa'uld home-world. Yet. Second, we do not serve the Goa'uld, and they are not gods."

"Well, of course not," Dane interrupted indignantly. "What do you think we are, some sort of primitives?"

Carter hid a smile. "You're no more primitive than we are, I promise." She laughed a little. "We might have more advanced technology, but that doesn't make you primitive, believe me."

"Well, of course not." Markhtin got up, went over to the sideboard, also elaborately carved in what seemed to be the favored tree motif, and picked up a bowl of fruit and a platter of baked goods shaped like houses and boats and animals. "I'm hungry. Will you eat?"

"I want to hear more about the Gates and the other worlds," Dane demurred, reaching automatically for the food anyway, taking the bowl from his brother and placing it on the table. Markhtin opened a door in the upper half of the sideboard and got out a pitcher and cups, placing them on the table as well. Carter refused to even look as he filled one of the cups, afraid she would see the lethal brown stuff again. "How were you chosen for this travel through the Gate? Here we have contests, tournaments and games to see who is the best. Do you? Markhtin and I competed together, because we are brothers. And we've won many times. Both of us are Candidates." This last was a matter of considerable pride.

"But perhaps only one of us will be chosen to go." This possibility clearly worried him. "The Choosing will be this afternoon in the market square," he informed the two team members. "That's so the Chosen may say their farewells to their friends and give away all their possessions, because the Goa'uld provide all they need."

"We'll both go, or not go," Markhtin assured him. "Our mother went," he added to his silently appalled visitors. "She was very beautiful, and very wise, and she was Chosen, and when the Rejected Ones returned they told us she had been Accepted by the Goa'uld. She won everything she competed in. Have you won often?"

"Uh, we don't exactly compete to visit the Goa'uld," Carter said, feeling ill, and not only from the vestiges of hangover. She reached for a sample of the bread to cover her reaction. It was sweet and crisp, a light yellow, tasting of strange spices.

"I want to know what they're really like," Dane went on, as if he hadn't heard her, "and what really happens once one is Accepted."

"They live like kings," Markhtin said through a mouthful of bread. "We already know that."

"How do you know that?" Carter challenged.

"The Rejected Ones tell us so." He swallowed, washed down the roll with a long drink of what Carter devoutly hoped was water, and picked up a small knife to peel a reddish-yellow fruit. "Alizane, Jareth, even Karlanan. They've been there. You haven't. So I believe them. They tell us it is a wonderful world, very strange, with streets of gold and perfumed air. And there are many people there, all in service to the Goa'uld."

"Why do you call your rulers Rejected Ones?" Teal'C spoke for the second time, startling all of them. Somehow they had managed to lose track of his looming presence.

"Because they're the ones that aren't Chosen," Dane answered hesitantly. "And they get sent back, and they bring us gifts. The Goa'uld are very powerful, you know." He laughed. "But of course you know. You've seen them."

Carter stared across the table at him and his brother. They were typical young men, indistinguishable, except for their clothing, from thousands of college freshmen back home. They ate with young men's appetites, unconcerned with the bread crumbs sprinkled over their tunics. And Markhtin, at least, showed no fear, none at all, of the subject of their discussion.

"Do your Rejected Ones tell you what happens to the Chosen?" she asked softly.

"What?" Dane was more apprehensive than his twin, but eager too.

"They're chosen to serve them," Markhtin said after a moment. "They're happy. It is a great honor."

"The Goa'uld are using your people," Carter said.

"Well, of course they are," Markhtin mumbled through another mouthful of food. "It's part of the agreement. Because we allow them to Choose, they don't destroy us. And sometimes they give us things. We're very lucky to be able to serve the Goa'uld."

"A long time ago, they threatened to destroy us," Dane explained. "So we came to this agreement with them, and the Chosen keep the rest of us safe, and we live in peace and plenty." He chewed vigorously and swallowed. "To be Chosen is a very great thing. Some of us the Goa'uld Accept—they're the most honored of all. But even the Rejected Ones, those who come back when their time of service is finished, are greatly honored. Our rulers come from among them. So you can see that it's a great thing to be a Candidate."

"Do you know what they Choose you *for*?"

The boys looked at one another uneasily.

"What do you mean? We told you already—to serve them." Dane said at last. He rubbed at his eyes as he spoke, as if something irritated them.

Carter shook her head and took a deep breath. "The Goa'uld are not human, like you and me. They only appear that way because they're parasites. They take your Chosen Ones and they invade them, inhabit them like worms, take over their minds and bodies. They need humans as incubators for their young, as hosts for their mature forms. They're monsters."

The boys stared at her, Markhtin's mouth hanging open and revealing half-chewed scraps.

"You're mad," he said at last, swallowing. "That's impossible. It's monstrous. It's a fantasy."

"Our mother would never consent to anything like that," Dane added, rising to his feet. "You must be insane. Go—"

"If we show you proof, you will believe us?"

"It's a lie. There can be no proof of a lie."

Carter sighed and closed her eyes briefly. She liked these kids very much, and she wished there was some way to avoid what they were going to see next. But they deserved to know the truth. "Teal'C."

The black man stepped forward, and the two boys got up and backed nervously away. "What are you doing?"

Teal'C laid his energy staff on the long wooden table and loosened his wide leather belt. He was wearing a wraparound tunic over Army issue khaki pants, and as he parted the cloth, pulling it free of the belt, Dane stepped closer to his brother.

"What is he doing?"

"Watch," Carter said. She wanted to turn away, to avoid even a glimpse of what was coming, but she had to look and not be afraid—for Teal'C, who was her friend and ally, as well as for these two naïve children who had no idea what was coming.

Teal'C pulled the tunic open without saying a word, exposing a dark, massively muscled abdomen with a curious X-shaped orifice overlying where his navel ought to be. The boys stood frozen, horrified, even though the opening didn't bleed.

The flaps of skin pulsed back and forth, and Carter swallowed bile.

The X darkened, spread, everted, exposing red inner tissue.

A white, questing tube of independent flesh issued forth from the gaping hole in Teal'C's stomach. At first it looked like a piece of intestine, but it was smoother, thicker; the blunt end opened in a tripartite yawn, revealing a pale gullet. The thing twisted and turned, blindly seeking, and tendrils stretched out from it, yearning toward the two boys.

"This," Teal'C said impassively, "is a Goa'uld larva. It was implanted in me when I was a child. The Goa'uld implant them in the Jaffa because they cannot exist for long without a host body. The larvae mature within our bodies and then, when they are ready, they transfer to other hosts, which they take over completely, obliterating the personality of the new host entirely. This is the true reason the Goa'uld demand tribute from your people: to supply such final hosts. This is the purpose to which you will be put. If you are fortunate, you will become merely a slave. If you are not, you will be possessed by an adult Goa'uld and sentenced to a living death."

The larva squealed, as if in anger, and withdrew into the big man's belly. Teal'C sucked in his breath as the creature pulled back and the slits closed to mere lines once more.

The two boys stood, wide-eyed and pale, staring at the crossed slits; and then Markhtin spun and lunged for the door.

He didn't make it in time. His brother held his shoulders as Markhtin vomited again and again, staining the polished floor and painted wall. In between his heaving, they could hear him whimpering, brokenly, one word over and over. *"Mother!"*

Carter and Teal'C exchanged impassive glances. At least their demonstration had definitely made an impression.

"The others," Dane said, looking back over his shoulder at the visitors, his face gray as his twin sagged to the floor. "We have to tell the others."

# CHAPTER SEVEN

"Heeeeeere dialer dialer," O'Neill crooned. "Come out come out wherever you are."

Jackson glanced at him and sighed deeply. O'Neill had a bad habit of going off on bizarre tangents under stress. One learned to play along.

"Got any better ideas?" the colonel inquired, feigning offense.

"Oh, I don't know, maybe you could set up a box trap with tacos?"

"You just don't do topical sarcasm well, Daniel." The two of them were standing once more by the M'kwethet Stargate, systematically surveying the area around it. They had gone into every open shop around the square, looking for anything that might be a DHD—"anything bigger than a bread box," as O'Neill put it. The idea of actually asking everyone they met about the missing control panel was one that they had mutually dismissed, at least for the time being. Or at least O'Neill had dismissed it; he seemed to feel that it would reveal a serious tactical vulnerability. Daniel himself had no problem with asking directions. In the process of searching, they'd also acquired more information about M'kwethet, its technological level, its potential trade goods, and its food. The people they'd met were polite and friendly, curious but not intrusive; they thought their visitors were very unusual but nothing to be particularly afraid of. Daniel had mentally tagged several as potential future informants. From an anthropological point of view, it had been a very productive morning.

A bit of minor haggling—Daniel had brought along some small, exquisitely engraved plaques for trade purposes—had produced meat and vegetables wrapped in a soft flat bread, reminding them both of burritos. O'Neill had asked for the extra-hot salsa, which had only gotten them more confused stares.

Still, the food was good, and hot even without the salsa; much better than field rations. They had repaired to the Gate to eat it and had just finished the last few scraps; now they were enjoying the view of the city, sprawled within its bowl of hills, spread out before them. It was a pleasant respite from a growing worry.

"What are we going to do if we can't find it?" Daniel asked after a long, aching pause.

"Stay here," O'Neill replied bluntly. "And that's not an alternative."

Of course it wasn't. But what if, Daniel wondered. What if this was the place that the Goa'uld came to retire—never mind that they hadn't actually found any Goa'uld on this world—and what if Sha're came through—

He allowed himself a moment to fantasize about it. This time, this time she would recognize him. She'd reach past the Goa'uld that possessed her—never mind that "nothing of the host remains"—and they would find some way to get rid of it without killing her, without even hurting her. He'd find a way to take her back to Earth, or maybe they'd just stay here, they'd be safe, happy—

"We'll find it." O'Neill's absolute assurance interrupted Daniel's reverie. "It has to be here somewhere. We just haven't looked in the right places yet."

"Maybe Hammond'll send a team after us."

"Nope." O'Neill didn't look at him, merely continued to survey the city from mountainous horizon to mountainous horizon.

"Why not? We've sent teams in before when contact's been broken."

"Into the middle of a town?"

Daniel thought about it. Say, SG-8, armed to the teeth, weapons ready, charging to the rescue, through the Gate and right in the middle of the vegetable auction.

Well, maybe, but it was unlikely. Hammond wasn't the type to declare war on vegetables.

"A probe, maybe?" Sending another probe—now, that was a logical thing to do. Come to think of it, of course that's what the general would do. It wouldn't be a threat to the inhabitants, and SGC could gain intel from it without risking lives.

Of course, even if Hammond did send another probe, it wouldn't get them out of here. It would only allow them to let the General know what had happened to his people.

O'Neill didn't sound very enthusiastic about the idea either. "You plan to sit here and wait?"

Well, that *was* a drawback. He shook his head.

"Didn't think so. So we're going to keep looking. The control has to be here somewhere."

"Well, it must be a lot farther away from its Gate than any other DHD we've ever run into. I didn't think it was possible to have one so far away."

"I didn't think it was possible to walk on other worlds in my lifetime," O'Neill said. "But here we are."

"Well, you've got me there." Daniel half-sneezed. "But dammit, every place we go there's pollen. Why is that?" He sneezed again and then coughed, clearing mucus from his throat. "I hope this isn't a cold instead."

"Just lucky, I guess. You should apply to the Guinness Book of World Records as the person allergic to the most planets." O'Neill paused in his absentminded banter to sharpen his attention on a figure making its way across the square to them. "Oh, look, teacher's coming."

Daniel looked up from fumbling for a tissue to see the

lithe figure of the female Rejected One crossing the square toward them. Last night, he seemed to recall, she'd been dressed appropriately for a head of state. Today her attire was much more practical and straightforward, a thigh-length brown tunic that left both arms and legs exposed. Her feet were bare. The visible flesh was nicely tanned. Her only adornment was a thin gold chain about one ankle. The noon sunlight danced in her hair, sparkling in the silver glints.

O'Neill, Jackson could tell, had noticed. He had that pleased, appreciative glint in his eye, the one he got around attractive women. He even got it around Carter sometimes when she wasn't looking.

Alizane marched up to the foot of the platform, put her fists on her hips like an outraged washerwoman. "I have been told you are asking questions of our people," she informed them. "What do you think you're doing?"

"Sightseeing," O'Neill responded promptly. "Nice town you've got here." He smiled, turning up the charm to full. "Nice people in it, too."

"Thank you." Her words were reluctant. Aware of it though she might be, she wasn't immune to his effort, and a smile struggled to express itself in return. Jackson thought of it as one more example of a profoundly polite culture—even a termagant couldn't entirely overcome her conditioning. "Is there something in particular you are seeking on our world?"

O'Neill's teasing grin vanished. "We told you that already," he said. "We're looking for help against the Goa'uld."

Her expression sobered too. "And we have told you, you won't find that help here. We've reached an accommodation that has worked for our world for centuries past counting. There is no reason for us to help you. I'm sorry, but when your people call for you, you must go back."

"That's the other thing we're looking for," Daniel said,

pushing his glasses up on his nose. Enough already of this frantic discreet searching. "Where's the control panel for this Gate?"

Alizane pulled her attention away from the colonel with difficulty and looked at him blankly. "The what?"

"Daniel!" O'Neill growled. The more-than-half-flirtatious grin had long since vanished from the colonel's face.

But it was too late anyway. "The control panel. With the symbols on it. What you use to select the Gate destination. Where is it?"

"I don't understand what you're talking about."

She really looked like she didn't understand, which made no sense at all. But then, the request the night before hadn't seemed to register either.

"How do you control the Gate destination?" O'Neill demanded. As long as the cat was out of the bag—or somebody else was willing to ask for directions—he was flexible enough to change his tactics and pursue the question.

It had to be a façade, Jackson decided. Had to be. That whole I-don't-need-to-ask-for-help thing was about as real as the colonel's flippancy and sarcasm. Like those two traits, it had a tendency to evaporate once the chips were down.

"We control nothing," the woman answered, as if baffled by the very possibility. "The Goa'uld open the Gate." She looked from one to the other of them. "And so do you, I suppose. Does this mean we will have to deal with your people, too?"

"We *aren't* the Goa'uld," O'Neill said between his teeth.

Several of the people in the marketplace, attracted by the exchange, had casually wandered over and stood behind their Councilor, giving the two team members the feeling they were facing the beginnings of a mob. A polite mob, perhaps, but a mob nonetheless.

"Even if you aren't Goa'uld, what will *you* demand from us?" Alizane bristled. That was the core of her antagonism, Jackson realized suddenly. She knew they weren't Goa'uld, but apparently whatever came through the Gate had to be more powerful than the M'kwethet, and she was worried about what that implied. He felt a sudden flash of sympathy for the belligerent woman.

"We don't demand anything." O'Neill's hackles were rising too. "Except that you stop dealing with the Goa'uld."

"You're fools." She stepped up on the platform beside them and spread out her hands, indicating the audience, the square, the whole vista stretched out before them. "Look at our city. This is what our sacrifice wins us— peace. Comfort. An opportunity to grow."

The audience murmured agreement.

"Neville Chamberlain would be proud of you," the colonel snarled.

"Who?"

Daniel stepped in, wishing he had a bucketful of ice water to throw over them both. "How do you know when the Gate will open?" he asked her, trying to defuse the conversation. "How do you know when the Rejected Ones are coming back?"

She regarded him with a certain gratitude, apparently preferring to talk rationally with him instead of the colonel. At least Jackson wasn't demanding that they turn their entire way of life upside down. "They send us a message through the Gate. One of the Jaffa comes. This allows us time to prepare the celebration and choose the new tribute. When you came, at first we thought you had been sent with such a message. Now—" She shrugged helplessly.

"So you don't have the capability to control the Gate from this side at all?"

"Why should we? The Gates are a thing of the Goa'uld.

We have no need of them ourselves; the Great Ones use them to take our tribute."

"How can you do this to your young people?"

She laughed softly, bitterly. Her voice dropped so as not to carry to the assembled watchers. "Do to them? We ask nothing of them we have not been through ourselves, do nothing that hasn't already been done to us. Only those who return through the Gate can be a part of the Council and choose the new tribute. Only those who know."

"And you still do it?" Jackson was trying very hard to keep accusation out of his voice. But it really *was* a conspiracy, he thought. A conspiracy that had been maintained for generations.

"Of course we do." Her gaze shifted to O'Neill, traveled over his uniform. "Your friends call you colonel. Why?"

"That's my rank. I'm a military officer."

"Your world has military? Wars? Famine? Plague?"

"Yes."

"The Goa'uld save us from all that."

"At the cost of what—twenty kids a month?"

She sucked in her breath, managing to control her initial response, and said calmly, "Once. Now it is only every two years. You are fortunate to have come in a year of Return and Selection. Those who are selected are greatly honored, because they are willing to lay down their lives for their people. Doesn't your world consider that an honorable thing to do?"

"They couldn't maintain twenty a month," Daniel murmured, fascinated in spite of himself. "Not unless some of them got chosen more than once."

He also noted, absentmindedly, that all the attraction that had existed, however momentarily, between Alizane and Jack O'Neill had long since evaporated. Neither party appeared to miss it.

"Fortunate? Honored? If you don't mind," O'Neill said evenly, "we'll state our disagreement for the record. And we'll get the hell out of here as soon as we can." Jackson could recognize the signs: O'Neill had made up his mind and was going to cut his losses.

Alizane shrugged, looking relieved. "So long as there aren't more of you out there to interfere with us, you can do whatever you please."

"Oh, there are a lot more of us. There are more worlds out there than you can possibly imagine. But I doubt anyone else 'out there' would give you the time of day. They wouldn't have anything to do with quislings either."

Alizane didn't get the reference, of course. "Then we can agree on some things, can't we? Both you and I will be well pleased to see you go." Glancing at the Gate, she added, "It won't open again until the day after tomorrow, our Returned Ones tell us. When it does, only the ones you hate so much will come through. You may wish to reconsider your position unless your own people come for you. But until then, I request that you stay out of our way. We have matters of our own to attend to."

As she turned and walked away, O'Neill protested, "They're committing suicide, that's all. They're marching through that Gate—they're sending kids through that Gate—to die. How can they do that?"

Daniel searched his memory. "Well, you know, there's precedent. Not just the legend of the Bull of Minos, but ritual suicide in Japan over matters of honor. Suttee in old India. It's well established in many human cultures." There was another Earth analogy, too, that had to do with twelve million people hoping that if they stood quietly in line their tormentors wouldn't hurt them, but they had been wrong, too. He decided not to bring that one up.

"Bull," O'Neill said firmly. "It's appeasement, and appeasement never works. One of these days the Goa'uld are going to come in here and wipe them out, and they'll never be able to figure out why."

Apparently the colonel remembered the same analogy.

\* \* \*

It was late in the afternoon when the citizens of M'kwethet began to gather again in the marketplace for the Choosing. Karlanan showed up first, using glares to herd O'Neill and Jackson away from the Gate, and then set up a small table with the yellow-and-black pottery bowl he had carried so carefully before. Off to one side a large brass gong was set up, and when everything was in place, Karlanan struck it, twice.

The sound reverberated through the square, shivering in the awnings, bouncing off the high hills surrounding the town. The two Earth men grimaced and moved farther away, back against a wall, trying to keep the Gate platform clearly in sight.

"I wonder where Sam and Teal'C are," Daniel murmured.

"That thought has occurred to me, too," O'Neill growled. They had expected the other two to show up much earlier, and had remained at the Gate as the agreed-upon meeting place. They'd gotten used to the stares of the natives, and after a while the natives had gotten used to them too. Even the kids no longer found the strangers fascinating; they weren't doing anything interesting.

The square filled rapidly in response to the summons. Once again people stood and sat on the flat roofs and the second-story balconies. The previous day's flowers were wilted and trampled, reflecting somehow the changed mood of the occasion. This time the crowd was silent, waiting. The only empty space left was directly in front of the Gate platform, and the crowd had edged back from it as if fearful of contamination.

Karlanan, the cynosure of all eyes, waited until there was barely room for the audience to move, and then struck the gong again three times.

The people pressed back, jostling each other, to make a pathway between the Agora and the platform. O'Neill found himself separated from Jackson by several bodies, but the other man was able to turn and acknowledge him. At least he wasn't likely to be able to charge forward in this crowd, O'Neill thought, for all the reassurance that brought. Daniel might try to keep the peace in conversations, but under the right provocation, he also had a tendency to let his emotions run away from him and do some *extremely* risky and extremely unpredictable things.

He craned his neck to see if he could spot Teal'C and Carter. They hadn't seen the others since they'd gone to talk to the kids Carter had met the night before. He was feeling a little uneasy about them, though he doubted that anyone on this world would try to take on Teal'C, and anyone who tried to manhandle Carter was in for a substantial surprise. Still, with what looked like a very significant percentage of the population of the town—maybe even the world?—right here, there wasn't any reason for them to be missing. The kids they'd been talking to ought to be right here with everyone else.

He could see Jackson glancing around uneasily too. Great. If the scientist was getting nervous, that meant he wasn't just kidding himself. There was a possibility of real trouble here.

And what if the Gate opened right now? If Hammond did send another probe through? They'd lose their chance to escape; he wasn't going to leave half his team stranded on this world. There weren't any guarantees they would be able to get through again.

Though maybe he could send Daniel back to explain matters while he rounded up the rest of the team. He allowed himself a moment of self-exasperation at letting the team split up, and then let it go. It was the best decision he could have made at the time. Who would have thought there'd be a world with no DHD?

Well, he *should* have thought it. But that was hindsight.

But there *had* to be a DHD. How else could this world "send" its tribute? The only thing that could go the "wrong way" through a Gate was radio waves. There had to be a way to open it from this side.

As he strained to see, a procession began to issue from the portico of the Agora, up the hill. A whisper swept through the crowd, as if each person had contributed to a collective sigh, and then they were silent again.

Leading the procession were about two dozen young men and women, dressed in identical white tunics trimmed with red. They walked in pairs, their lines ragged, as if no effort had been made to rehearse the moment or match sizes or strides. They carried sistrums, strings hung with bells and stretched between two pieces of wood, but they made no attempt to play them. The bells chimed softly, erratically, with their footsteps. O'Neill thought he recognized some of them as the young people joined by Jackson and Carter the night before. A quick glance at Jackson elicited a confirming nod. So the kids at that table had been set aside for a reason. These were the Candidates for Choosing. That fit with Carter's request for further contact.

And maybe the captain had succeeded. The ragged rows didn't look happy about being in their little procession. As they came down the slope to the square, he could see faces paler than usual. Apparently, O'Neill thought, the honor of it all had escaped them. Or at least a few of them had had serious second thoughts. As they came closer, starting up the steps to the platform, he thought he could see tension, nervous swallowing. The sistrums quivered from more than the vibration of footsteps.

As the audience got a look at them, some voices were raised as if in protest, followed by a collective "hush" by their neighbors.

Behind the double line came the dozen or so Rejected Ones they had watched return through the Gate. Today they were robed in bright, cheerful colors, blues and greens and yellows, as if a mobile flower garden proceeded down the path. Their faces were a study in conflicting emotions. A few kept their expressions as immobile as possible. The others vacillated between nervous laughter and attempts to be somber. O'Neill was nearly sure he spotted at least one tear rolling down a sun-bronzed cheek.

Last of all came Alizane and Jareth, who wore a gown and cloak literally covered with real flowers. The perfume poured across the first few rows of spectators. The older Council member looked sad, but nodded every few steps to acknowledge the crowd. The crowd, for its part, nodded back, but made no sound at all.

Alizane, oddly enough, was still dressed in the brown tunic, as if she hadn't had the time to change into more festive attire. Her mouth—and a very nice mouth it was, O'Neill still admitted—was tight with fury. The last of the sunlight, catching the red highlights in her hair, made her look like a volcano in the process of erupting. Her gaze swept across the crowd as if she were looking for someone, and he pressed back against the wall, letting the people in front of him obscure her vision.

The space in front of the platform had been filled by the young Candidates. The Returnees made their way up the steps to the platform, followed by the two Council members.

As they sorted themselves out, a minor disturbance in the crowd behind the colonel attracted his attention. He managed to turn enough to see Carter's blond head as she worked her way through the crush, using elbows and hands as required. Several of her victims yelped in pain before squashing themselves against their fellows to give her passage.

"Captain, so nice of you to join us," O'Neill murmured. "Adopted the native clothing, I see. Looks good on you. Where's Teal'C?"

"He's . . . elsewhere, sir." She was panting, as if she'd run, but spoke softly, glancing meaningfully at the people around them, who were still shooting resentful glances at her. Somewhere along the way her uniform had been abandoned for the mid-thigh tunic belted at the waist and leather sandals that most women on this world seemed to prefer. "We've got a problem, Colonel. I think you'd better come with me."

"It's going to be tough to get out of here for the next little while," he pointed out, speaking just as softly. "What's going on?"

"Not here," she shook her head, glancing around nervously at the crowd and the assembly at the foot of the Stargate. "Sir, we've got to get Daniel and go. Now. Please."

"Well, since you asked so nicely . . ." He raised his voice. "Yo, Daniel!"

Daniel had barely managed to turn when Alizane, who had heard the call as well, pointed at them from the platform.

"Stop them!"

"Get out of here, Captain," O'Neill said instantly. "That's an order."

All around them, people were looking around uncertainly. Their attention was attracted immediately to O'Neill and Jackson, whose Earth clothing made them stand out. Jackson gave O'Neill a resigned look as the men and women surrounding him pressed in on him.

O'Neill chose to struggle, in order to give Carter a better chance to escape in the confusion.

Before he fell, he thought he saw her slip away.

# CHAPTER EIGHT

Escape was impossible, and there was no point in trying to kill people just for the sake of proving how tough he was. Besides, if he didn't fight too hard, maybe they wouldn't either.

It sounded good in theory, but in practice there were some problems. He'd accumulated a goodly number of bruises by the time they dragged him and Jackson to the foot of the M'kwethet Stargate. Nothing disabling, fortunately; while the crowd had obeyed Alizane, they had no idea what was going on and hadn't really had their hearts in it. And Carter seemed to have gotten away clean.

Jackson was thrown down on the paving stones next to him. There was so little room that they were practically nose-to-sandal with the Rejected Ones.

Jareth and Alizane were arguing quietly but fiercely on the other side of the Gate; he could see them framed in its circle. Karlanan stood by the gong, game but confused. Muttering rose from the crowd.

Finally Alizane and Jareth came around to the front of the Gate. O'Neill pushed himself up on his knees and sat back to look up at her. Out of his peripheral vision he could see Daniel do the same thing. Damn, Jackson hadn't even lost his glasses in the struggle.

Alizane still looked furious, but when she raised her voice to speak to her people her voice was carefully under control.

"People of M'kwethet, we gather here as we have gathered for all our history for the honor of Selection. What we ask of you we have given; what we receive you shall share."

"Generous," O'Neill commented. Karlanan kicked him in the kidneys, then stepped around his pain-contorted form to hold the ceramic bowl at arms' length to Alizane and Jareth.

"We choose blindly," Jareth said, reaching into the bowl, taking a small white cube, and placing it on the table behind them.

"We choose fairly," Alizane said, and took another cube from the bowl.

O'Neill was afraid they were going to announce every single selection with yet another self-excusing platitude, but Jareth took the next cube in silence. They alternated, one after another, until they had drawn twenty cubes from the bowl and lined them up neatly on the small table.

The silence from the watching crowd was oppressive. A foot in the middle of O'Neill's back pressed him down against the stone platform.

Karlanan shook the bowl, producing a small but distinct rattle.

"We have not lost everything," Karlanan announced, completing his part of the ritual. "Some still remain."

"Better luck next time," O'Neill whispered through clenched teeth. Jackson made frantic *shut-the-hell-UP* faces at him.

"Let the Candidates come forward," Alizane ordered.

"Bring on the empty horses," whispered O'Neill. Karlanan kicked him.

She picked up one of the cubes, holding it high so everyone could see, and handed it to Jareth, who examined it and called out a name.

From the crowd, someone screamed—a man, O'Neill

thought through a haze of pain. The foot removed itself from his back, and he sighed in relief.

A teenage girl stepped forward, ashen-faced, and Alizane embraced her and led her to one side.

The process was repeated. Another girl, who by her looks couldn't have been more than fifteen, joined the first.

Then a boy, another boy, another girl.

Then Jareth read out a name, and no one came forward.

By this time O'Neill had levered himself back to his knees and was able to see the panicked look the older Councilor gave Alizane before repeating the name.

Still no answer.

The crowd rippled.

Jareth took a deep breath and shouted the name one more time, so loudly that his voice cracked. "Markhtin Baker's-son!"

Karlanan shook his head from side to side. "Choose someone else," he rumbled.

"No!" one of the remaining Candidates protested. "Why should one of us have to take the place of one rightfully Chosen?"

Other voices from the remaining Candidates rose, agreeing. Jareth's lips tightened, and he ostentatiously set the cube to one side, by itself.

Alizane picked up another cube, hurriedly, as if to pretend that everything was proceeding smoothly and nothing unusual had happened.

"Verais Silksmith," Jareth announced.

It was the name of the protesting Candidate. She shrieked and lunged for him, grabbing at the cube. At the same time a bellow of protest came from the crowd, and several of Verais's relatives, obviously believing Jareth had called their little girl's name to punish her for her impertinence, surged forward. A few of the Candidates still unchosen tried to stop them. O'Neill was nearly certain it was one of the selected ones who took the opportunity to sweep the bowl and the stack of cubes already drawn off the table, scattering them across the platform. He glimpsed Jackson snatching up a few, and took the opportunity to palm some himself. Maybe they could fix the ballot in some small way.

Alizane was beside herself, yelling and kicking at the melee. Her face was a study in panic. Jareth was somewhere behind a wall of red-trimmed Candidates; Karlanan was on his hands and knees desperately searching for the little cubes, shielding the jar with his body.

Jackson materialized by O'Neill's side, pulling him to his feet. O'Neill gasped as a rib jabbed, and then set his jaw, putting the pain aside until there was time to worry about it. They'd made their way down the shallow steps and almost into the crowd when Alizane spotted her prisoners making their escape and sent her Returned Ones after them.

"Get out of here, Daniel," O'Neill snarled. "Find Carter and Teal'C."

"I'm not leaving you here."

"The hell you're not—"

But by then it was too late, and their squabbling had delayed them enough that the Rejected Ones of M'kwethet had captured them again.

In the hills above the town, Carter and Teal'C shepherded six frightened teenagers up and away from the city walls. The six, four boys and two girls, cast equally terrified looks at their back trail and at Teal'C, who provided their rear guard.

"Captain Sam," Dane said as they paused, "What will happen to us?"

Carter wiped her mouth with the back of her hand, staring at him, stalling. She hadn't the foggiest damned idea what was going to happen next, she realized with a shock.

When the twins had recovered from their initial terror at the sight of the larval Goa'uld that occupied Teal'C, they'd insisted that their friends needed to know the truth, too. Carter had been all for it. Teal'C had kept his opinion to himself, though once Markhtin and Dane had located some of the others and persuaded them to come to the little house on the Bakers' Lane, the Jaffa had obligingly induced the larva to show itself once more.

Some of the teens had reacted in exactly the same way the twins had. But a few, to Carter's consternation, had steeled themselves against the sight of the parasite. They had lifted proud heads and proclaimed that they were willing to do anything, even be taken over by that thing, if it was necessary to maintain the peace with the Goa'uld.

It couldn't be all that bad, one of the boys had reasoned. Teal'C didn't seem to be harmed by it.

When they tried to explain the difference between carrying a larva and an adult Goa'uld, the holdouts had seized on the information that the larva kept its host healthy and long-lived. Besides, they saw no reason why they should believe that being possessed by an adult Goa'uld was any different then carrying a larva. There was nothing in the little room to convince them. Besides, if a larva kept one healthy—not a very great inducement, apparently—what powers might an adult bestow?

Carter had refrained with effort from leaping across the room and shaking them silly. When one of the Candidates pointed out that it was time to gather at the Agora for the Choosing ceremony, the holdouts leaped at the opportunity to leave.

But they had left behind the twins, and the other four, two boys and two girls.

"What do you want to do?" she'd asked.

"Run away," Dane said immediately. "Now. Before the Choosing. Far away so they can't find us."

This idea was greeted with universal acclaim, until Teal'C pointed out that as strangers on this world, the Earth team had no idea where they could run.

Markhtin assured them he had an idea, and Carter made him promise to gather provisions while she notified O'Neill.

The remaining candidates looked at each other.

"The others will tell them what you told us," Dane said. "I don't know what the Council will do, but they won't be very happy that their lies have been exposed. I expect they might try to kill you all."

"Then they'll just have to come with us," Markhtin responded. He'd been green about the gills, refusing to look at the larva the second time or even remain in the same room when it made its appearance. He'd come back in only when he was assured it had withdrawn, and he still sniffled from time to time, casting sideways glances at the Jaffa.

Then Clein'dori, a slender blond girl who radiated common sense, pointed out, "If you're going back to the Agora, you can't go dressed like that. They'll see you immediately."

Dane looked confused. "So? They've already spoken to the Council. Why should it matter now?"

"Because," Clein'dori explained in long-suffering fashion, "the others will tell the Council why they're late and why some of the Candidates aren't there." This was followed by considerable shuffling and trading until between the two girls, and with a little help from the boys' mother's wardrobe, they found enough spare bits to provide Carter with something resembling a disguise. She hoped no one looked too close. The others had scattered too, agreeing to meet back at the house on the Bakers' Lane as soon as possible with the required provisions.

Then O'Neill and Jackson had been taken, and Carter saw no option but to gather her little flock and flee.

Now they were sitting on the slope of a hill some four miles from the city, catching their breath.

"What do we do now?" Dane repeated. "What will happen to us?"

Carter took a deep breath. "I have no damned idea," she admitted.

The kids migrated toward each other, like sheep huddling for security.

"Has this ever happened before?" she asked. "Have any of the Candidates ever not appeared for the Choosing?"

A moment's mumbled consultation, and Clein'dori stepped forward. Of all the town dwellers, she was the only one to have provided herself with a walking stick, a long sturdy gray staff. She leaned on it now.

"My mother told me that once, long ago, there was a sickness in the city, and some of the Chosen sickened before the Gate opened for them. The Council of that time did not know whether to send them or not. Finally they decided not to, since it would be an insult to the Goa'uld to send less than our best."

"What happened?" Teal'C asked, in a tone that said he knew very well what happened.

"The Goa'uld came through the Gate and threw the bodies of the Chosen into the marketplace, and slew all their families. They said that their agreement was for a certain number that year, and they would not take less.

"The Council tried to explain, and the Goa'uld slew them too, and then went from house to house in M'kwethet, dragging young and old, babies and granddams into the street, and made their own selection, double the number that had been agreed upon for that year, and they burned the houses and the shops and the shrines. The Serpent Guards took our people away.

"Two seasons later, when the Rejected Ones returned,

they brought with them the cure for that sickness, and all others like it, and word from the Goa'uld that never again would plague be permitted to interfere with the selection of the proper number of tribute.

"And so it has been from that day to this," she finished, as if reciting a saga taught from generation to generation. "Never again has sickness taken hold in M'kwethet. Never since has a tribute counted short. Our agreement has been honored."

"Until now," Markhtin muttered, sitting on a rock and looking back at the whitewashed walls far below. He rubbed at his nose.

"Until now," Clein'dori agreed. "But perhaps none of us would have been Chosen in any case."

"And there are enough left to make up the numbers," Eppilion, one of the boys, piped up hopefully.

With a part of her mind Carter hoped that they realized the ethical dilemma they had created for their fellow candidates and themselves. Another, more selfish part said that at least these six would be safe. And if it were true that a person could be a Candidate only once, then once the Choosing was over they would be safe forever. She couldn't save them all, or at least she couldn't think of a way to save them all. Particularly not those who, having had the chance to see what a Goa'uld really was, still reported in. In a way she had to admire their courage, if not their common sense and gift for self-preservation.

That wasn't her issue now. She had to hide these kids for at least a few more days, and she had to get O'Neill and Jackson out of M'kwethet.

Once the team was back together they could tackle the issue of getting back home again.

Captain Samantha Carter, Ph.D., USAF, took a deep breath and wondered what her mother would have to say about all this.

Well, since it was Mom who got her that Major Matt

Mason doll—with the cool backpack that made him fly; what was a doll without the proper accessories?—her mother would be in no position to tell her daughter that she should have skipped the Ph.D. and gotten the MRS. instead. Of course, how could Mom have known that astrophysics would lead to what was beginning to look like a serious case of kidnapping?

Enough dithering, she told herself sternly. "Markhtin, you said you knew a place where we could hide. Lead on. Teal'C, you take rear guard. Once we get settled we'll go back for the colonel and Jackson."

Markhtin led the way up the stony path, away from the overlook. Carter and Teal'C cast a wary glance at the sky overhead, where dark clouds were gathering, and the Jaffa moved off, seeking a place where he could find cover and still watch the back trail.

The wind was picking up, spraying dust behind them. At least with this much air movement it wouldn't hang in the air behind them. One of the kids coughed; Carter couldn't tell which one. Tree branches began whipping back and forth, and something blue and furry bounced across their path.

At least she didn't have to worry about being too out of shape to keep up. Years of training allowed her to follow them without even getting particularly out of breath. She had leisure to study the six of them as they climbed deeper into the hills.

Markhtin and Dane, the twins, always stayed close together, as if supporting each other, even though their personalities were very different. Markhtin wore brighter clothing, kept his hair trimmed shorter, was the first to speak and the last to concede a point. Dane was far more withdrawn. Even now he seemed more frightened, drawn into himself, while his brother hovered protectively and surreptitiously lent him an arm over the bigger rocks in their way.

Eppilion was small and dark and intense, usually quiet, and every time Carter had laid eyes on him, he'd had a wine stain at exactly the same location on his tunic, no matter whether he wore ceremonial white attire as a Candidate or casual clothing. Carter couldn't figure out whether that meant he was consistently sloppy or had consistently bad luck when he drank.

Clein'dori had a theatrical flair, demonstrated in the way she had immersed herself in her story. It seemed to be balanced by practical hardheadedness; she used her staff with the skill of long practice, proceeding to the head of the line with brisk attitude. When she had to stop and wait for Markhtin to indicate which path to take, Carter could practically hear her drumming her fingers with impatience.

The other two candidates, Yahrlin and Maesen, were a quiet pair. The only thing they seemed to be definite about was that they wanted no part of Goa'uld larvae in any way, shape, or form. Maesen couldn't even bring herself to look at Teal'C. Yahrlin simply avoided looking at anyone, as if profoundly ashamed of running away.

The sun had long since set, and the afterglow was nearly gone from the sky, when Markhtin finally paused and pointed up to a dark spot on the slope far above them. "Up there," he said between pants.

Carter followed his gesture and scanned the slope, looking for the way up. "All right," she said. "Getting up there in the dark is going to end up with somebody breaking a leg. We'll make camp here and go for it in the morning."

# CHAPTER NINE

"There is a difficulty," Teal'C greeted her with the sunrise.

Carter groaned and rolled to a sitting position, rubbing her eyes. This world didn't even have coffee; she didn't want to hear about difficulties at this point. She wanted to hear about hot bubble baths and good food and a soft bed and warm blankets. And no decaf.

Oh, well. Maybe in her next life.

"What is it?"

"Two of the children are sick." Teal'C sounded a bit unsure of himself—a rare occurrence. Because the Goa'uld larva he carried conferred an exceptionally high level of immunity, he himself was never sick. Before the larva had been implanted he'd been subject to all the ills humanity was heir to, but that had been a very long time ago. "I do not know if they can travel."

"What's going on?" she demanded, crossing the area to the blankets spread out on the ground. The others crowded around behind her silently.

The sick ones were Markhtin and Maesen. Their eyes were closed, and a film of sweat covered their foreheads, but they were trembling as if with cold. Carter wasn't a medical expert, but she'd had enough field training to recognize fever when she saw it.

"What is it?" Dane asked, and as she glanced up at him she realized that all of them were looking to her as the person with all the answers. It was bad enough when adults did that; kids actually expected you to have answers for life's little tragedies. "What's wrong with my brother?"

"He's sick," she said, feeling foolish, "I don't know why. Did they eat something different from the rest of you?"

"No." Even the levelheaded Clein'dori sounded frightened. "They woke in the middle of the night. They complained of aching in the head, and they coughed and sneezed, like your friend. Then they lay down and wouldn't wake up."

Like Daniel? Could the kids have caught Jackson's cold? Did Jackson have a cold this time, instead of the ubiquitous allergies?

And if that was the case, then they had a viral infection, and there wasn't anything she could give them to cure it. Maesen and Markhtin might be the first to succumb, but the rest of them would certainly come down with it too.

And if they didn't have resistance to the common cold, it might actually kill them. According to the story they'd heard the day before, the Goa'uld had taken sickness away from this world. Now the Earth team, putative allies against the aliens, had brought it back.

Carter took a deep breath. "All right," she said, with far more certainty in her voice than she actually felt, "this is what we're going to do. We need to get them under shelter, probably in that cave up there. We're going to keep them warm, make sure they get plenty of liquids and rest. And we'll stay with them until they're well again." She thought about mentioning the analgesics in her pack, glimpsed the incipient panic in Dane's eyes, and decided against it. There weren't enough to go around, and Dane was far too likely to jump to the conclusion that any medicine she carried was supposed to work miracles. She'd hang on to the little bottle of aspirin and hope they could work through the infection and pain without it. "Let's go."

It took several hours to get the two sick teens up to the cave. The last part required Teal'C to carry them, one at a time, cradled in his arms up a path so steep that it made Carter particularly grateful they hadn't tried it in the dark. He disappeared into the cave for the second time, and then his voice echoed out at her.

"Captain Carter. You must see this."

She scrambled up the last bit and was startled to find a bright, steady illumination coming from deeper in the cave. Following the path of the light, she slipped and slid down a narrow passageway to find a high, arched pocket in the earth.

As she brushed dirt out of her hair—the passageway had a low ceiling—she looked around to see lamps glowing in several niches in the walls. Polished metal set behind them and angled toward the roof provided indirect lighting. Clein'dori and Yahrlin moved briskly around, lighting more lamps, while Teal'C was settling Markhtin in an actual, real cot against the rough stone wall.

The two casualties were covered, Carter noted, with warm blankets. For a refuge in the wilderness, the kids had done pretty well for themselves.

"Are we going to die?" Eppilion asked in a very small voice, catching sight of her.

Teal'C interposed a question. "What about Daniel Jackson and Colonel O'Neill?" he asked. "Should we go at once to inform them?"

Getting back to her feet, she shook her head. "We can't bring this sickness back to the city. It's going to have to run its course and they're going to have to develop antibodies before we can go back. There's too much risk." She took a deep breath and looked around at the refugees still on their feet. "The rest of you should know that you might get sick too. This is a common thing on our world, a trivial illness that only lasts a few days." *I hope,* she thought. "I want you to tell me if you start feeling chills or if your head hurts or you have trouble breathing. Meanwhile, I need to know what we have available here to help us."

"Maybe we should have gone to the Choosing," Yahrlin said fretfully. "We're being punished for running away. The elders told us we had to live up to our responsibilities, and now look."

"You aren't going to die, dammit," Carter snapped, hoping desperately that it was true. "This isn't any big deal. It's just that this is a new sickness for you, and your bodies have to learn how to fight it. We're just going to stay here for a little longer than we planned, that's all."

Maesen, lying at her feet, coughed and groaned.

"Somebody give them some water and cool cloths for their faces. Yahrlin, Eppilion, you're elected. Clein'dori, Dane, I want some answers. What is this place, where did all these supplies come from, and who found it?"

Teal'C, watching her take command, didn't ask his question again. Meeting his eyes, she knew it was still going through his mind as well: What was happening to the rest of SG-1?

That was a totally different bridge, and they'd cross it as they came to it. For right now, she had to keep six kids alive and under control and in quarantine. There was always the possibility that Daniel had infected half of M'kwethet already, of course, but that wasn't something she could deal with now. One problem at a time. One piece of one problem at a time.

She marched Clein'dori and Dane back over to the nearby table and sat down with them. The wooden chair creaked under her weight, and little puffs of dust escaped from the joints, but it held. The young ones were a bit disconcerted when Teal'C joined them. His chair creaked even louder than the others.

"Okay," Carter repeated, "what is this place? You knew it was here, didn't you?"

Markhtin's twin cast a worried glance back toward his brother before answering. "We all knew about it—"

"There were stories," Clein'dori corrected.

"All right, there were stories." The young man looked annoyed. "We used to tell each other about a place up in the hills where our people would go and hide when the Goa'uld came, before we made our peace with them."

"So this is that place?"

"Not exactly." Clein'dori picked up the tale, oblivious to Dane's irritation at having it taken away from him. "There were only stories. But some of us liked to go explore in the hills when we were young, pretending it was the old days. We found some of the places where our people hid, and we brought more things up here."

"So the Council already knows all about this place and they're going to show up any minute." Carter felt like throwing her hands up in the air and giving up, abandoning them. If they were going to run away, did they have to be so obvious about it?

"Oh, no!" Dane was shocked. "It's a secret. We've never told anyone about it."

"That was part of the game," Clein'dori added. "In the old days, there might be traitors. So we were very careful."

No doubt these kids thought they were the only ones ever to invent this particular game based on ancient oral tradition. It never occurred to them that every generation of potential Chosen had heard the same stories and had gone hiking in the same hills. Judging by the age of some of this furniture, Carter was willing to bet that the supplies in the hill caves had accumulated over decades. Alizane, Jareth, and Karlanan might even have brought some up here themselves.

"If they have not come yet, they may not come at all," Teal'C rumbled, echoing her own thoughts.

That was a possibility: The Council might choose to adopt a posture of official ignorance in order to allow a few of the more volatile members of their society to believe they had an outlet for escape from the biannual fate of their people. According to what Carter had picked up in discussions with Jackson about cultures and how they served the needs of their members, that would make sense.

Or maybe they really didn't know. Maybe the kids were right and it was all a carefully kept secret. After all, the Council was made up of those who didn't run away from the selection, so maybe they had never been let in on the secret by the few who actually had the courage, or the cowardice, to run away.

And if that were the case, there were probably search parties combing the hills for them at this very moment.

Carter had to remind herself that there was no evidence that M'kwethet was able to field large numbers of organized search parties. They weren't an aggressive people; the closest to this kind of situation they might have to deal with would be lost children who wanted to be found, not people who were deliberately hiding. The stories were very old, after all.

"All right," she said. "Here's the plan. I assume there's a good source of water in this cave?"

Clein'dori nodded vigorously.

"And there's food. Okay. We're going to stay up here until everyone is healthy again, and then we're going to go back to the city."

Dane looked frightened suddenly. "They'll punish us."

Clein'dori was exasperated. "Of course they will. So what? No matter what they do, it'll be better than . . ." she glanced at Teal'C and stumbled into an embarrassed silence.

"I understand," he said reassuringly. "And I agree."

From across the width of the cave came a long, harsh series of coughing and a moan. Carter winced. Next time they were going to have to do a better job of physicals before they ventured onto a new world.

Always assuming there would be a next time, of course.

Always assuming that the team would be reunited, and able to get home again.

Assuming. She hated assumptions. They were nasty treacherous unproven things and they'd trip you up every time.

They'd be okay, Carter told herself. It was just a matter of camping out for a few days, and they had food. They'd be fine.

"Speaking of water," she went on, "what does a girl have to do to get a drink around here?"

For a place that appeared to be peaceful, agrarian—downright bucolic—M'kwethet had a reasonably sophisticated detainment facility, O'Neill thought. Not only was it considerably cleaner than the usual dungeon, but how many dungeons sported white marble floors anyway? High-quality marble, too, with lovely light-gray veins tracing through snowy stone.

Veins.

Maybe they wouldn't want to get their floors all messy with blood and stuff.

He could hope, anyway.

Stretching, he set his weight against his left arm and pulled. This turned out to be a mistake, as he'd suspected it would; the metal cuff around his wrist bit deep, and the short chain fixed to the wall didn't give an inch. He tried again with the other arm just to be sure.

Now his wrists had matching bruises.

He was chained in a small alcove, able to see directly in front of him but not to either side. The level of light was comfortable enough, though he couldn't identify its source; no flickering, so probably not firelight, and besides, he couldn't hear crackling or smell burning. His field of view included part of a door, an empty alcove opposite, and in between a wide expanse of floor interrupted by thick columns carved in a spiral pattern, and a highly polished, new-looking wooden table with cuffs at both ends and a large wheel for a headboard. It reminded him irresistibly of a rack. Maybe that was one of the innovations the Goa'uld had gifted their slave stock with?

Not even an enraged mob was able to do too much damage to his fatigues, but the remains of his shirt had been cut away by the Chosen, the Rejected, and the rest of them, the better to aim their blows, no doubt. It was all very cliché. Any minute now Maleficent would come barreling through the door, long fingernails twitching for his eyes.

"Daniel?" he yelled. "Daniel, can you hear me?"

Holding his breath, he listened.

Wind: he could hear the wind, so there must be a window nearby, and he couldn't be too far underground. All the dungeon traditions said there ought to be water dripping somewhere, but he couldn't detect it.

He couldn't hear anything else, really. Just the wind. No background noises, no marketplace sounds, no restless movement of guards. Just wind, and the cheery clanking of chains. Most certainly not an answer to his call.

"Daniel!" he bellowed once more.

Nothing.

How likely was it that he was the only prisoner in all of M'kwethet? Come to think of it, the metal staples holding the chains to the wall *did* look shiny and new.

Not very. It wasn't likely that the people of an alien world had built a marble prison just in case Jack O'Neill from Earth should stop by, start a riot, and need chaining to a wall all night. He didn't think his reputation had spread *that* far.

Although if it had, the marble was certainly a nice touch.

No; time to quit being snide and think. Assess the situation.

First, start with his physical condition. Bruises aplenty, a loose tooth and a nicely swollen lip. Rather surprisingly, no broken bones, not even ribs. He took a deep breath, as deep as possible, expanding diaphragm and rib cage to their fullest, and got no more than a mild warning twinge. Okay, maybe a cracked rib. No big deal.

Headache, from concussion. That happened when you got knocked out. His vision wasn't blurry and he wasn't too dizzy. Again, no big deal.

Muscles: sore, getting stiff. Being chained to a wall had distinct disadvantages, particularly when it went on for several hours at a time. His shoulders were beginning to burn from the tension—he was holding his arms up in order to relieve the pain of the iron cuffs. Still, if he could just get loose, he could do whatever he needed to do.

Weapons? Nope. They'd taken his pack, his gun, the works. He probably didn't even have the knife in his boot anymore; that familiar pressure was gone.

That left the team. Where the hell was Daniel? Given his own relatively untouched condition, he couldn't believe they'd killed the archaeologist. The people of this world might have an Alizane or a Karlanan here and there, but for the most part they were just too meek to show that kind of aggression. Daniel wouldn't be dead. That must mean he was being held somewhere else. M'kwethet was a small place, so it couldn't be too far away.

Carter and Teal'C—well, he had to trust that the other half of the team ("the better half?" a little voice in the back of his head inquired ironically) had made it away clean. Carter'd said there was a problem. Most likely it was related to the missing Candidates; Markhtin was one of the ones she'd been talking to.

Operating theory: Carter and Teal'C had persuaded at least one and maybe more of the Candidates to skip the Choosing. That would account for her needing to talk to him and for the fact that at least one she'd met had chosen not to be Chosen. Based on the reaction of the crowd, this didn't happen very often, and the idea of picking somebody else to take the missing kid's place didn't go over well at all.

Obviously the Council members thought he was involved. So he could expect interrogation. Well, he'd done that before, and it was nearly his least-favorite team sport in the whole world—his eyes squeezed tightly shut in an involuntary effort to banish certain memories. It almost worked. He allowed his mind to veer away into more ironic analysis, but the little voice that never really went away pointed out that as a defense mechanism, irony had its weak points. It was really rusty in places, in fact.

And his operating theory could be full of used cattle feed. Jackson, Carter, Teal'C, all of them could be dead because he'd failed to spot the missing DHD. The Council could be coming, with the knives and snakes and acid—or worse, his opinion about the nature of the people here could be dead wrong, and they could have captured and be torturing the rest of his team. His responsibility: the grimly efficient Jaffa, the naif archaeologist, the infuriatingly scientific captain, screaming . . .

He could hear his own breath coming in harsh, angry pants, and he grabbed back control of himself. He wasn't going to let his imagination run wild. He wasn't going to lose it over a few chains, he told himself firmly; why, handcuffs could be taken in a whole different context sometimes. He tugged again, experimentally, but the fixtures didn't give any more than they had the last time.

He was getting thirsty, and it had been a long time since that burrito in the marketplace. So it had been several hours, maybe even all night, although he didn't think he'd been out that long. The light level was frustrating; he couldn't tell anything about the passage of time.

One of the tricks of interrogation was making the victim want to see the interrogator, if only for the company. Damned if he was going to fall for that one.

*"Daniel!"*

* * *

Elsewhere in the stone palace that was the center of government of M'kwethet, Daniel Jackson woke to find himself lying in a firm bed with a soft pillow, between cool, rough-woven linen sheets. For a moment he imagined himself back on Abydos, and turned to seek Sha're.

Sha're, of course, wasn't there. What was more, the very act of turning his head triggered a pounding headache and reminded him of other impact points all over his body. Daniel took a deep breath and closed his eyes. When he opened them again, his vision was clearer, and Jareth of the Manyflowers was leaning over him, a blurred look of concern writ over his kindly face.

"You're awake."

"Well, yes." Why did people always say such idiotic things, he wondered, and then gave a mental wince. Clearly he'd been around Jack far too much. "Yes, thank you."

Jareth nodded and indicated a small table next to the bed. It held a simple pewter cup (*Oh, they've got alloys,* the archaeologist in him noted) filled with what looked like water, a plate of fruit and odd-shaped bread, and, he was grateful to see, his glasses. "It is morning now. Would you like to eat?"

He was, Daniel discovered, ravenously hungry. Still, he levered himself up cautiously, well aware of fleeting aches and pains, reaching automatically first for the glasses and blinking. The look of concern snapped into focus. Once upright, he started to take a sample of the fruit and then stopped himself. "Where's Jack?"

A look of pained disgust wiped away Jareth's concern. "Your friend is elsewhere. He isn't harmed, I assure you."

Daniel swung his feet around the side of the bed, covering himself with the brown-threaded, cream-colored sheet. It really was very much like the cloth of Abydos. "Can I see him?"

Jareth sighed and seated himself in a carved wooden chair beside the bed, facing him at an angle to allow Jackson access to the table. "Not yet. We have a terrible problem, and you must help us."

"What kind of problem?" Jack would be exasperated at him, but he couldn't help it. He always responded to problems by trying to help. It would get him killed one day, Jack lectured him. Maybe today was the day. "And why can't I see my friend?"

"Your friend is not inclined to be cooperative," the older man said, smiling at his own understatement. "For his safety, and our own, he is held elsewhere. Please, eat."

"Not inclined to be cooperative." Well, that could describe Jack O'Neill sometimes. Daniel found himself tearing a piece from the loaf of bread (not much sand, the academic in him noted; that would help account for the generally good shape the natives' teeth were in), thought about it, and decided to go ahead. Starving himself wouldn't help. He was careful to sniff the water before drinking, but it smelled exactly like water, and he wasn't at all sure he could detect any drugs anyway.

Jareth waited patiently as Daniel chewed and swallowed, finishing the bread, peeling and sectioning the tart fruit and devouring a couple of pieces of that as well before resuming the conversation.

"What kind of problem do you have?" Daniel repeated, finishing the last of the water.

Jareth refilled the cup from a plain gray pitcher before answering. "The Choosing has never been disrupted before as it was yesterday. It was a disgrace. Some of the Chosen were not even present. Tomorrow the Gate will open, and the Chosen must be ready. Where are the missing Candidates?"

The bread and fruit threatened to make a reappearance. Daniel swallowed hard and pushed the glasses up on the bridge of his nose. "You mean the kids you're sending to the Goa'uld."

"Yes."

"I'm afraid I can't help you with that. I won't do anything that involves sacrificing human beings to the Goa'uld."

"You don't understand," Jareth pleaded. "We must fill the tribute. This is our way, has been for more than a thousand years. It keeps us safe."

"Yeah, you're safe, and they're being sent straight to hell."

Jareth straightened as if slapped. "What do you mean?"

"Do you know what happens to your tribute once the Goa'uld get their hands on it?"

The older man got up, began pacing nervously from one end of the small room to the other. His sandals slapped on the marble floor.

"Of course I know," he said, waving his hands to punctuate his words. "I myself was a Candidate. I was Chosen, and I was sent. I have been where they are going. I am a part of the Council, I conduct the Choosing, only because I myself have been Chosen. I am one of the Rejected Ones, sent back by the Goa'uld to maintain the tradition."

"And the supply of new hosts for Goa'uld larvae, and zombies for Goa'uld adults?" Daniel asked acidly. He couldn't block out of his memory the last time he had seen Sha're, the evil blankness behind the eyes he loved. And these people submitted their children to that *on purpose*?

Jareth stopped in midstride and stared at him, mouth open. He opened and closed it a few times before he found the words he was searching for.

"What is . . ." He stopped, thought better of it, and began again. "You don't understand. That is the risk we take, the price we pay for our peace and freedom. We must do this, otherwise they'll destroy us."

"Has it ever occurred to you to fight?"

"They would destroy us." The words hung in the air between them, simple, unanswerable. "Rather than have us all die, we send them a few. And of those, some nearly always return home.

"But they will destroy us, unless you tell us where the missing Candidates are."

"Sorry, can't help you." Daniel felt a sneeze coming on as a breeze found its way through the little window. His head was feeling a little stuffy, too. "Look, I want to see my friend. Now. Where are my clothes?"

Frustrated, Jareth shook his head. "You don't understand. You have to help."

"Nope." Daniel felt his answer was almost O'Neill-like in its brevity. Jack would be proud of him.

Other issues were beginning to make themselves known, however. He had to have the signaler, the device that opened the iris on the Gate back home. If they ever found a way to dial home, the iris had to be open. What had the Council done with it?

Most of all, and immediately, he needed a bathroom. He wondered if the Goa'uld had provided their zoo animals with running water.

Apparently they had. Once Jareth understood his question, the older man nodded briskly and pointed to what looked like a side wall. In fact, it was an alcove, containing an actual sink with faucets and a utilitarian hole in the floor. Another faucet above the hole served to flush waste away.

He'd seen worse, in places alleged to be more civilized than this one.

His clothes and belongings, however, were another matter. Jareth declined to provide any information on their whereabouts. After some debate on the subject, Jareth left Daniel standing in the middle of the room, wrapping the sheet about himself for what warmth and modesty it could provide.

*What would O'Neill do in a situation like this?* he wondered.

Whatever it was, Daniel was certain that the colonel wouldn't let a little nakedness stop him.

# CHAPTER TEN

"Your friends are dead," Alizane announced, with no pre-
liminaries. "We found them in the hills this morning and
killed them. Where are the Candidates?"

O'Neill tilted his head to one side, examining the female
Councilor. He was damned tired and no longer concerned
with maintaining the pristine state of the floor. His arms
hurt, and he wasn't even a little interested in the attrac-
tiveness of the woman before him, not even a little impressed by the pair of bodyguards accompanying her.
"Bullshit."

Alizane blinked. "I beg your pardon?"

"That's a word we use on our world to tell people we
know they're lying," he explained kindly.

One of the bodyguards hit him, rocking his head back
hard against the wall. Well, he'd seen that coming. He
rubbed the blood from the corner of his mouth off on his
shoulder and tested cautiously for more loose teeth. Nope,
not this time. He hadn't even lost the one that was already
wobbly. The guy had absolutely no talent at all. In fact, he
was rubbing his knuckles surreptitiously, as if he'd hurt his
hand on O'Neill's jaw.

"The Gate opens tomorrow morning," Alizane said, des-
peration coming through in her voice. "The Candidates
must be found."

"Well, hey, if you need to make up the numbers, why

don't you volunteer?" he jeered. "After all, you've been there before. No big deal, right?"

As soon as the words were out of his mouth he regretted them. There was nothing like putting ideas in their heads, was there? From the look of sick terror that flashed through the woman's eyes, he could tell there was no way she would ever go back to the Goa'uld. They'd have to come after her and drag her back, kicking and screaming.

But they couldn't drag her *back*.

There *had* to be a way to open the Gate from this side.

He'd had lots of time, hanging in chains all night, to try to figure out how to get out of this one. Try as he might, he could think of only one way.

"You said the Jaffa came through the Gate to tell you when to get the tribute ready. You're sure it was a Jaffa, not a Goa'uld?"

Alizane snorted, whether at the implication she didn't know the difference or at the role reversal of prisoner interrogating captor he couldn't tell.

"Tell you what," he said, speaking rapidly in order to put the proposal on the table before his own sense of survival cut in. "You need to make up the numbers, right? We're not going to give you the kids. But if you give us our clothing and our packs, Daniel and I will go instead."

Her mouth was open to shout at him again. She closed it, staring at him incredulously.

"I mean it," he urged. "Send us. You know what it's like there—you don't really want to send the kids into it. You don't really want to lose anybody, do you?" He hoped she wouldn't realize that she was the one who held all the cards in this hand. She was hesitating, thinking. Behind her, the two guards moved restlessly, and she held up a hand to silence them.

"Come on," he urged. The chains clanked as he moved forward, pushing his idea. "Look, what have you got to lose?"

If the Jaffa could open the Gate without a DHD, then he could too. All he had to do was watch, follow, find out how they did it.

Then they'd have a chance to get Carter and Teal'C back, too. He hoped.

Of course, that depended on a lot of things happening exactly right on the Goa'uld world. But at least it was a chance, however small, however crazy, and it was something he could influence.

One step at a time, he reminded himself, holding his breath as he watched the woman chewing her lip. A deep line drew itself between her brows as she considered it.

"The Candidates," she said. "What about the Candidates?"

"The kids will show up after the tribute gets sent. They'll be safe then, right? No reason for them not to come home." For one crazed moment he thought about offering to import Jimmy Carter with a full pardon for the deserters, but he managed to restrain himself better than the chains did.

"When the Goa'uld see you they'll know we failed." She was considering the idea, at least. About to reject it, maybe, but considering it.

"Not if you give us some idea what we're walking into," he argued. The chains rattled again. "Come on, Alizane, you don't want to sacrifice those kids either. You don't want to put them through what you went through." He was repeating himself now, but only because it seemed to be his strongest argument. However much the Council prattled about how honorable it all was, they didn't really *want* to pay tribute. They just couldn't see any other alternative.

Once again, she flinched as his words hit home. "We do this because we must." She was almost pleading for understanding now and unconsciously confirming his assessment. "Not because we want to. It is necessary to safeguard our lives, our way of life. Surely you can understand that."

What he understood, O'Neill thought, was that these

people were just not seriously into this torture business. Not that he objected to that part, of course. But they also rejected anything that hinted at real suffering. Maybe that was why they were so willing to accept Goa'uld domination—no intestinal fortitude.

"No, I don't understand," he snapped, letting his anger show despite himself. "I don't see how you can close your eyes to what happens after you send those kids through. And I happen to think that freedom is worth fighting for."

"It isn't worth the death of all our people." The platitude seemed to give her strength.

"Just some of them, right? Well, you'd *better* add us to your tribute then, because we're not going to give away your kids."

"Enough." She raised an exasperated hand. "Enough!"

That afternoon the Council of the Rejected Ones of M'kwethet met in formal session, behind the closed doors of the centermost room of the Agora. Most of the day had been taken up by an intensive debriefing of the Returned, in a ritual effort to try to discover as much as possible about the Goa'uld. As always, there was nothing new to tell. They went through the Gate. It was cold. They saw great wonders. They served. Some were taken away and never came back.

It never changed.

Nonetheless, upon returning, the Rejected Ones were intensively debriefed for every possible snippet of information about the Goa'uld they could recall. Out of every group that returned, perhaps half would commit suicide within a year, unable to manage the memories they did have.

Now they were considering a new problem.

"Were you able to find out where they've taken the missing Candidates?" Karlanan challenged his two co-

Councilors. His fists were resting on the table, and he was hunched over them, knotted with intensity.

"No," Alizane and Jareth answered at almost the same time. The three of them looked at each other and at the pile of otherworldly items stacked on the table between them: strange metal rods, boxes, cloth bags, knives.

"Why not?"

"I don't think they know," Alizane added. "The other two must be hiding them up in the hills somewhere. One of them is a Jaffa, so perhaps we shouldn't look very hard."

"I don't know what to advise," Jareth admitted.

"We have to find them," Karlanan growled low. He lunged to his feet, fast enough that Alizane, sitting opposite, pushed back startled in her chair. "We can't send a short tribute. We have to have the full twenty."

"The O'Neill suggested that he and Jackson could go instead," Alizane said, her voice uneven. "He seems to think he'll be able to . . . I don't know what he thinks he'll be able to do. I'm sure he has some plan, though."

"Whatever plan he has will probably get us all killed." Karlanan's eyebrows drew together, and his lower lip twitched. "I think we should kill them ourselves, maybe send the Goa'uld their bodies, with an explanation. And we should find those six and send them all, to teach the others that they can't evade their duty. What if next time everyone refuses to be Chosen?"

Jareth and Alizane nodded soberly. "We can't afford to set a precedent," Jareth said. "But at the same time— perhaps we can pretend that nothing is wrong if we just send those two outworlders instead. It isn't as if the Goa'uld actually pay any attention."

The other two shared a wryly reminiscent glance with the older man. Each of them had been Refused from a separate Choosing, sent back as insufficiently attractive or interesting or healthy for the Goa'uld that season. Perhaps they'd just not met some completely different, thoroughly alien criteria. Over the centuries M'kwethet had tried to figure out what the Goa'uld wanted, in order to stave off their fury. They'd never figured it out. Once or twice the entire contingent of Chosen had been Returned, contemptuously, and shortly thereafter, each time, death had reigned over the city. Once the entire contingent had been Selected, and no one had been Returned at all. That occasion was still marked by an annual day of mourning.

"I don't think we should send the Goa'uld dead bodies," the woman said thoughtfully. "They might take it as a challenge, perhaps."

Karlanan snorted. "They know we would never challenge them. We're not insane."

"But apparently there are some worlds out there with insane people," Jareth interjected, reaching for some of the strange, shiny metal objects the strangers had carried. "They actually think they can fight, perhaps even win. Maybe they can."

The other two stared at him. After a moment Jareth smiled sheepishly, letting the heavy metal object fall back onto the table with a solid *clunk*. "It's nonsense, of course. Forgive me for even suggesting it."

"Karlanan, what progress have you made in finding the Candidates?" Alizane turned away from the older man and back to Karlanan, refusing to even acknowledge Jareth's temporary aberration. "You sent out the searchers. What have they found?"

"Some of the missing took food and clothing," the younger man answered grudgingly, similarly ignoring Jareth. "Not much, though. Their parents and sibs, at least the ones who witnessed their going, all said they were in a hurry, but at least three said they would be back soon."

"Soon, as, in time for the opening of the Gate?"

Karlanan shook his heavy head. "There's no way to know."

"I suspect they plan to wait until after the Gate opens

and closes again before they'll return to the city." Jareth was still trying to recover from his earlier remarks. "They'll think they're safe then."

Alizane shook her head. "From the Goa'uld, perhaps, at least until they come through to punish us. But how shall we deal with them? We have to do something."

"Kill them." Karlanan was single-minded. "They must be punished."

"Perhaps it would be better to spend our time planning how to hide from the Goa'uld," Jareth insisted.

"How to hide—" Alizane stopped in midsentence to look at the older man, who suddenly flushed deep red beneath his gray beard. "Oh, no. Surely not."

"What?" demanded Karlanan.

Alizane and Jareth were still locked in each other's gazes, and so Alizane managed to catch the tiny shake of the head Jareth gave her. When she broke the exchange she carefully did not look at Karlanan. "Nothing. Nothing at all.

"I think we ought to take our visitors up on their willingness to volunteer to take the places of our Chosen Ones," she went on determinedly. "I think we ought to Choose them, in fact. They should go as part of the tribute, and then let us forget them.

"The others will be back, I'm sure. But I will vote against killing them. If the visitors take their place, there's no reason to punish them so long as the tribute count is met."

"And what of two years from now? What if the Candidates run away then, too? Will we have visitors from other worlds available then to take their places?" Karlanan was on the verge of an explosion.

"If it happens again two years from now, we will find a way to handle it then. We can take that time to better teach the young what their duty is." Jareth tried to placate the younger man.

"With the others walking around to show them how easy it is to avoid being Chosen? They'll have to die," Karlanan insisted. "They'll have to die in shame, so everyone can see it's worse to run away than it is to be Chosen for the sake of our people."

Alizane and Jareth looked down at their hands. "We'll deal with that later," Jareth said. "Not now."

Meanwhile, Samantha Carter leaned over one of the rough cots, smoothing damp, dark hair away from Maesen's forehead. The young girl coughed, the force of it lifting her from the surface she lay upon, her head rolling from side to side. Even without a stethoscope, Carter could hear fluid sloshing in the girl's lungs.

Several feet away, Dane sat beside his twin, patiently feeding him pieces of fruit picked fresh from trees growing near the cave. Carter had tasted it; it had the sharp taste of citrus. Maybe it was jam-packed with Vitamin C and an instant cure. At least Markhtin seemed to be doing a little better. Carter had tried feeding Maesen the fruit too, but the girl had slapped her hands away and muttered unintelligibly.

"She needs to sit up," the captain told Yahrlin, who stood nervously nearby. The boy nodded and continued to stand, wringing his hands and staring at his sick friend.

"Well, go get something she can lean on!"

Yahrlin jumped and fled. Moments later he returned with a large pillow. Between the two of them they managed to lift Maesen up, set the pillow against the wall, and lean her back against it.

She didn't appear to know what they were doing, but at least she breathed a little more easily. "Keep talking to her," Carter told the boy. "If she seems to come out of it, try to get her to take some water with fruit juice in it." She got up, wiping her hands on her tunic, and went outside, looking for Teal'C.

"I don't think she's going to make it," she told her colleague in a low voice. Teal'C was sitting beside a tall tree, taking advantage of the shadow, watching their back trail.

He nodded soberly. "I agree. The boy may recover, but the girl will probably die. Have the others become sick?"

She shook her head. "No, just those two. I know Maesen was sitting next to Daniel at the banquet, but so was Clein'dori, and she isn't sick at all. Their immunity levels must be really different."

"Perhaps Maesen is particularly susceptible."

"Seems like it." She ran her hands through her blond hair. "I don't feel like I can leave them, but I really want to know what's going on with Daniel and the colonel."

"I would be recognized if I returned to the city," Teal'C pointed out.

"I know. It's got to be me. But I'm going to try to stay with the kids at least tonight. I gave her the last of my aspirin an hour ago, but it doesn't seem to have helped much."

Teal'C looked up at her, his usually stolid expression revealing sympathy. "You are doing everything you can, Samantha Carter. Do not blame yourself."

"But she's just a kid," Carter replied, her eyes stinging at the unexpected comfort. "I brought her up here to save her, not to let her die."

"You are doing everything you can," the big man repeated.

"It isn't *enough*." She shook her head fiercely, as if to throw away despair. "All right," she went on. "Tomorrow they're sending the Chosen out. I'm going to be there, and find out what's up with Daniel and O'Neill. You'll have to stay here and keep an eye on the kids. Maybe we'll get really lucky and Maesen will have a miraculous recovery between now and then."

"Perhaps," Teal'C agreed gravely. But he was only

doing it to make her feel better, and it wasn't working at all.

The Chosen sat cross-legged on the floor before the members of the Council, listening hard. Occasionally they nudged each other and indicated O'Neill and Jackson, sitting at the back and sorting through their packs, looking for the signaler, their weapons, rations, and everything else they'd brought along. The Council had clothed the out-worlders identically to the rest of the Chosen. Jackson had worn similar clothing on Abydos and didn't mind in the least; O'Neill had decided that a miniskirt wasn't his look and couldn't figure out where to put his knees.

The two had noted with grim respect that the Council didn't have the most recent returnees present to answer questions; when the Chosen asked, they were told that the Returned were resting and celebrating with their families. It was a good way to keep raw, recent memories out of their reach.

"They had you *chained*?" Jackson asked for the third time, eyeing the raw circles around O'Neill's wrists. O'Neill was busy ignoring the question, slathering antibiotic cream on them and wrapping them with gauze from the packs. After a moment of watching the other man trying to wrap one wrist by holding one end of the gauze in his teeth, Jackson took it away from him and quickly made a competent field dressing. When O'Neill raised an eyebrow, Jackson informed him, "Learned first aid in the field. Not too many doctors on digs."

O'Neill grunted thanks and kept sorting. Whoever had searched his stuff had made a real mess of things. But at least it was all still here; he shook his head in wonder as his boot knife turned up too and slid it back into its sheath with relief.

Up at the head of the room, Jareth was talking. "When you go to the world of the Goa'uld, you will find it strange, but there will be those who will instruct you as to the proper behavior."

O'Neill grunted again, sarcastically.

"Tell me again about this wonderful plan of yours," Jackson prompted softly.

"If you can think of a faster way to get access to a DHD, you let me know." The answer came through clenched teeth. "If there isn't one here, and a Jaffa can come and go, they have to have portable ones. All we have to do is find one." He was beginning to have doubts himself, doubts that usually waited to make an appearance until some time after he found himself in deep kimchee, not before. This was not good.

The others around them glared, as if they were talking too loudly in a movie theater, and the Councilors coughed to regain their audience's attention.

"You will find that the servants of the Goa'uld will put you to work in familiar areas. I myself was a gardener." Jareth smiled, and the audience realized they were being prompted to chuckle. "The science of the Goa'uld is very great, and it is beyond our understanding. The wise among you will not seek to discover more about it."

O'Neill didn't have to look up to know that Jareth was staring directly at him.

"You will be provided a place to eat and sleep. For each tribute, it has been different, so we cannot give you more information about it."

*Yeah,* thought O'Neill. *Don't tell them about the crammed-into-a-dungeon part. It's a real downer.* He wondered if that bit of information meant that each tribute had gone to a different world. It certainly would be convenient if they ended up on, say, Chulak. At least they knew the neighborhood.

"Remember always that you go to serve, not the Goa'uld, but your world." He took a deep breath and began to step away from center stage, when a voice came out of the crowd.

"What about the larvae?"

O'Neill and Jackson exchanged glances. So Carter and Teal'C *had* spoken to some of these Candidates.

Jareth turned pale. Karlanan stepped forward to take his place. "I spent two years in service," he blustered. "I never saw these 'larvae' you mention."

Jackson snorted softly.

"We saw. One of the strangers has a giant worm in his belly. Ask *them*." Heads swiveled toward the Earth team members, and Jackson started to get to his feet. O'Neill grabbed his arm, pulling him down, and got up himself.

"What you saw was true," he said. "My friend Teal'C was a Jaffa, serving the Goa'uld, and he carries a Goa'uld larva inside his body." He was going to continue when his gaze met Alizane's. He couldn't figure out whether her expression was belligerent or pleading. Either way, she was making it clear that with one more word out of him the deal would be off. He continued standing, more than willing to engage in a stare-down contest with her, but kept silent. He'd told the truth. He wondered how the Council would spin it.

"That is for the Jaffa," Alizane said sharply. "None of you are Jaffa."

True enough, as far as it went.

"What happens to those who don't come back?" piped up another voice.

*Ah, the $64,000 question.* O'Neill allowed a small smile to play about his lips. He wondered how many times this question had been asked, and what standard answers the government of M'kwethet had developed for it.

"Some are Accepted permanently into the service of the Goa'uld," Alizane admitted. "This has never been hidden from you."

"Do they serve by being eaten alive by worms?" The

voice was shrill, and others in the group were trying to calm the speaker.

"I have never seen that," Alizane stated flatly. "Nor has Karlanan. Nor has Jareth."

"What about the Rejected Ones who just came back?" someone else demanded. "What have they seen?"

This time Alizane allowed herself to lose her temper, or at least appear to. "I have told you upon my honor that none of your Council have seen such a thing, and we were each part of a different tribute. Why should you think the latest tribute is any different? You're listening to aliens. Who knows if they're telling you the truth or not?"

The Candidates looked back and forth between their Councilor and the strange tall visitor from another world. Whispers rose and fell as they debated.

Alizane allowed the discussion to go on for a minute or two and then slapped her hand flat on the table. "Enough," she said. "Go and meditate. The Gate will open soon. You will need to dress in the proper robes; all else is being prepared. Remember you are honored to serve M'kwethet."

"Yeah right," O'Neill muttered, sliding back down and tugging at his tunic. "I hope the proper robes are more proper than *this* damned thing."

Samantha Carter pulled the rough brown cloth closer around her face, wrinkling her nose at the scent of raw lanolin. She leaned heavily on a rough stick, stumbling to the side of the alley to get out of the way of traffic. A shopkeeper glared at her and she ducked her head, pretending to examine the piles of dirt-encrusted brown vegetables in the shallow tray before her. She would have reached for a closer look, but her fingers were far too well manicured to be a native of this world. M'kwethet had not yet discovered pearlescent pink nail polish.

The merchant glared at her again. "Are you going to buy, old woman?"

Carter shook her head feebly and turned away. As she did so, a woman stepped into the street, calling her husband to close up the shop.

It was nearly time. Carter melted into the crowd and picked up speed, heading for the square.

She'd had a late start from the cave in the uplands, and had run the last six miles to the city, afraid all the while that she would arrive too late. She'd been relieved upon reaching the outskirts to find that daily life in the city appeared to be going on as usual. She'd had just enough time to catch her breath when the natives began a leisurely process of closing up shop.

Once again the open area of the market square was filling up from the edges in, leaving a path from the columns of the Agora to the Gate. The captain hesitated, then began working her way toward the columned portico. The kids had no idea where the Council might hold prisoners, but the Agora, like the building they named it for, seemed to be the center of government. It was a logical place to start.

The sun was high in the sky, throwing shadows almost straight down. Once in the shade of the portico, Carter let the robe loosen and fall back for a moment. Someone might spot the brightness of her hair, but the relief from the heat was worth the risk as she stretched and rotated her neck.

Voices from within the building caught her attention, and she reluctantly drew the robe up again and pressed back into a little alcove formed by a pair of supporting columns.

"I never was a cassock kinda guy, either," she heard a deep, sardonic voice say.

O'Neill? Easing her hand between the folds of the brown robe, she slid her fingers around the butt of her automatic and risked a quick peek around the column.

Not a dozen yards away, young men and women were

selecting piles of white clothing from a long table under the supervision of the Rejected Ones. Several of the Chosen were already undressing, slipping out of their outer garments and discarding them, pulling on the long white robes and belting them about the waist.

And sure enough, there was O'Neill, holding up a white robe by the shoulder seams. There was a bruise on one side of his face, and he was moving carefully, as if in pain. He lowered the garment and she got a good look at his mostly bare, welted torso. She couldn't refrain from a wince of sympathy.

Not far from him, Daniel struggled with a wide, colorfully woven belt, knotting and reknotting it, pausing in between to push his glasses up on his face. At his feet was his knapsack. At one point he knelt to rummage around in it, retrieving something to store in the fold of the belt.

Both men were barefoot. Neither seemed to be under any restraints, though the Rejected Ones, garbed in formal red, were watching them carefully when not helping the younger ones get dressed. The newly Chosen were keeping a safe distance away from the two men from Earth, not speaking to them, avoiding their gaze. Their body language made it clear that they didn't want to be associated with the strangers in any possible way.

She couldn't exactly come in blasting. Aside from the little detail of all the innocent kids around, she didn't have enough ammunition. Of course, the Council wouldn't know that.

Still she hesitated. There was something very wrong with this picture.

Holding her breath, she pulled the gun free and deliberately rapped the barrel twice against the stone column. The distinctive sound of tempered steel against stone chimed softly.

A few of the Chosen paused, looking up for the source of the strange sound. O'Neill laughed, said something low to one of the crimson-clad Chosen, and moved away, toward her.

Daniel looked up, confused, then at a silent signal from O'Neill asked the newly returned Goa'uld reject for help with the sash, stepping neatly between the M'kwethet and the colonel.

"Where are you going?" Karlanan said harshly.

"Just looking for a little privacy to change clothes in," O'Neill said smoothly. "People on my world don't usually strip down in public."

"Your friend had no problems."

O'Neill smiled painfully. "Oh, he's a scientist. They're expected to be strange."

"You must stay in sight."

O'Neill sighed theatrically and raised his voice just a little. "Look, Karl, we made a deal. We still don't know where our friends or your kids are, so Daniel and I are going in place of your kiddies. I'm not going to back out."

Carter couldn't stifle a gasp.

"I expect my people to protect those kids who don't want to go," O'Neill went on, still pitching his voice to the corners of the room. "In fact, if they were right here, I'd make it a direct order to keep those kids out of harm's way."

Daniel was staring at him, his hands still on the broad sash.

Carter was staring at him too, even though she could see only the colonel's broadly muscled back. There were some interesting scars there, she noted wildly, but nothing crippling and recent; that told her something about how he'd been treated, but . . .

"If they were here right now, in fact," O'Neill went on, "I'd tell them to bring the kids back once we were gone. Bring 'em back and await developments."

Developments? Had the man lost his mind?

"But they're not here," he concluded. "So I just have to

hope that somehow they get that message. We're not stealing your kids, Karl. But they're not gonna be Goa'uld chow, either."

Carter held her breath as Karlanan, fist clenched, moved closer to the colonel.

"Now, now, Karl. Modesty, modesty."

Karlanan growled.

O'Neill deliberately turned his back on the Rejected One and looked over the hem of the robe. "I'm glad my people aren't here," he said precisely. "But if they were, I'd order Carter to wait until after the Gate opens." He paused. "Daniel, you've got the bread crumbs, right?"

He couldn't find her in the shadows of the columns, she was nearly certain. But he knew she was there, somewhere. And he'd given her a direct order, if only she could figure out what it meant. Bread crumbs?

Laying a trail to follow home?

After a confused pause, Daniel patted his waist, over the broad, folded belt. "Right here."

So they must have the things from their backpacks. Their weapons, maybe? Even more important, the signaler?

The sound of tempered steel against stone rang out again, twice. Karlanan moved up on O'Neill, who waited until the other man was exactly one stride away to whirl in place and knock him sprawling. Accidentally, of course.

His solicitous murmuring, and Karlanan's enraged response, followed Carter she faded back between the pillars and out of the hall to join the crowd gathered in the market square.

From the anonymity of the crowd, she waited and watched as the procession gathered on the steps of the hall. This time the audience pressed itself back hard, out of the way, leaving a broad path from Gate to hall. She strained to see, among the Chosen, the taller figure of the colonel. He was the last to come out of the shelter of the portico, and as he turned to speak to Daniel, she could see a thin line of red disfiguring the white linen of his robe.

Daniel was the only one wearing glasses, of course. He didn't seem to be injured at all. He covered his face and turned his head away for a sneeze as O'Neill spoke to him.

The sun was high in the sky, directly overhead.

The crowd fell silent.

And then the ground began to shake.

Around her, voices murmured as if in prayer.

The shaking increased.

The Gate billowed open. A cry rose up from the crowd, a cry of awe and, perhaps, disappointment, as if they were hoping that maybe, somehow, this time it wouldn't happen.

The Gate stabilized, and through it marched a pair of Serpent Guards, their cobra-like helmets giving them a stature well over that of anyone in the cowering crowd. The two stood at attention, energy staffs held butt down before them. Their kilts and sandals evoked the pictures on ancient tombs.

Next came another pair of Guards, taking position just beyond the first two. The latest pair carried long trumpets, and as their cobra helmets split and folded into themselves, forming an elaborate collar around their necks, they raised the trumpets to their lips and blew, a long, shuddering, hollow note resembling the call of a shofar.

Absolute silence fell over the crowd.

Carter managed to pull her gaze away from the Guards long enough to glance at O'Neill and Jackson. The two members of the Earth team were staring at the Guards with grim, fixed expressions. The rest of the little party was silent too, although she could swear she heard someone sniffling.

Under the urging of the red-clad Council of the Rejected Ones, the Chosen were ushered into the wide path, toward the Gate and the Guards. The young ones stumbled, milling around, unwilling to take the lead. O'Neill and Jackson hung back, to lose themselves as much as possible among the rest. The crowd of Chosen passed close to Carter, nearly close enough for her to reach out and catch at the long loose sleeves as her teammates went by. She stifled the impulse to whisper something, a question, an encouragement, anything. They never looked around. The last few in the group pulled heavy carts heaped with cloth, pottery, metal, furs, gorgeous long feathers of a million colors, jars sloshing with oil, man-sized baskets of grain.

The M'kwethet tribute paused at the foot of the platform. The mournful horns sounded again, their echoes absorbed by the mass of watching humanity.

One more figure stepped through the Gate, this one clad in a richer material than the Guards. Instead of a cobra helmet, this one wore a white headcloth folded to form a triangular frame for the face, with lappets hanging down over his bare shoulders and a band of gold and turquoise holding it in place on his forehead. His eyes were outlined in kohl, heavily shadowed under thick, arched brows. His chest was bare over a kilt, also white, that fell in starched pleats to mid-thigh. The deep crossed cut that signified possession by an alien was stark upon his bronzed flesh. It meant that he was a Jaffa, not a Goa'uld, though the resemblance . . .

For one frozen moment Carter thought she recognized the figure. Then she realized that it was a stranger, shorter, more muscular than the last living image of a tomb painting she'd been unfortunate enough to see. Instead of the lethal ribbons twining about his hand and arm, the man wore a broad leather-looking brace on his left arm, laced together on the inside, extending nearly from wrist to elbow. She couldn't see all the details, but there was a large round gray thing in the middle and assorted bits of decoration studded around it.

Behind him, the Gate hissed into empty silence, and

once again she could see the buildings that formed the east
end of the square through the arch.

"Where is the tribute of M'kwethet?" the white-clad
man said, his voice splitting the silence.

"The tribute is here." It was Jareth, elbowing his way to
the head of the Candidates. "M'kwethet is grateful to fulfill the requirements of the Goa'uld. We bring the number
required, the best of our best, the product of our lands that
the Goa'uld have granted us."

The ambassador of the Goa'uld looked them over, Candidates and carts alike, as if they were all the same to him.
Carter held her breath as the dark gaze swept over the two
men so obviously older than the rest, but he didn't seem to
notice anything unusual.

"We will accept your offering," the ambassador said at
last. He touched a knob on the bracelet at his wrist, pointed
at the carts, and as if by magic a long ramp unrolled from
the Gate to the ground. He touched the bracelet again, and
stepped clear as the Gate's inner ring spun slowly back
and forth, pausing the requisite seven times before it
reopened behind him with a roar of unspace. Automatically, Carter memorized the symbols. Meanwhile the ambassador vanished through the gray surface without a
backward glance.

The Serpent Guards moved down the steps. Somehow
the four of them managed to overwhelm the Chosen,
herding them like sheep up the ramp. The people of
M'kwethet watched as their children groaned, pulling the
loaded carts upward, to the shimmering round blankness
that led . . . somewhere. The Guards made no effort to
help. When the carts slipped backward, they stepped backward, lowering the energy staffs to aim in the direction of
the struggling youngsters. Jackson stepped back to help.
So did O'Neill, though a grimace twisted his face as he
tried to push the cart upward.

One by one, before the silence of the crowd, the Chosen disappeared, stepping through the shimmering surface. Vanishing.

Through the Gate.

Into oblivion.

# CHAPTER ELEVEN

The space between worlds is cold, colder even than the guts of Cheyenne Mountain. O'Neill and Jackson were prepared for it, but even they were shivering as they stumbled through the Gate on the other side. The Chosen weren't so lucky; despite the fact that they had been warned in their briefing, many of them fell to their hands and knees, weeping from the shock. Their escort of Serpent Guards stood by impassively, apparently in no hurry to gather their charges and herd them to their ultimate destination.

They had exited the Gate into a great hall, one that made the Agora of M'kwethet look like a small lobby. A high, arching roof, held up by lotus-flower columns and spreading rib supports, was painted blue and figured with shining white clouds. The floor beneath their feet was a mosaic of millions of thumbnail-size chips of colored stone, forming a fantastic swirling pattern in glowing hues of blue. The walls were paintings, oddly two-dimensional, of men wearing kilts and double crowns surmounted with spitting cobras. They were seated on thrones, their hands crossed over their chests and holding crooks and flails. Behind each man so enthroned stood impossibly tall, impossibly lovely women, also wearing crowns, dressed in sheer pleated cloth and wearing broad, bejeweled collars. Their hands were outstretched to rest on the shoulders of the enthroned; it was difficult to tell whether they were entreating, supporting, or commanding.

Before the seated kings stood painted Serpent Guards, also dressed in kilts and leather-looking armor, their eyes red with a paint that glowed. Beneath the feet of the Serpent Guards knelt row upon row of men and women, dressed in apparel that ranged from raw furs to formal and glittering laces. Beneath it all ran a line of pictures and symbols.

Daniel Jackson polished the frost off his glasses and raised his head, the better to see the paintings. His lips were parted slightly, moving, as he studied them. All around him the rest of the Chosen murmured, shocked, and then fell silent as the hall took their words and threw them back in hollow echoes. There weren't enough other people around to soak up the sound: a small group standing by one of the hallways, debating animatedly; servants carrying trays to another arched doorway. It reminded Jackson irresistibly of reconstructions of the palaces of the pharaohs, only much, much larger and finer in every detail.

"Daniel?" O'Neill asked softly as he came up behind the other man. It was a warning as much as a question.

"Hieroglyphics," the archaeologist murmured. "Middle Kingdom or—no, that part has to be earlier."

"This might not be a good time," O'Neill went on more urgently.

Daniel looked up to see the Serpent Guards finally moving in on the huddled teens, keeping them together in a space away from the Gate. He and O'Neill were the only ones who had ventured very far away from the safety of the group. "Um, I see what you mean." The two of them casually drifted back to join the others. The Chosen watched them with wide, scared eyes, as afraid of the two strangers from Earth as they were of the Serpent Guards who stood at attention nearby.

O'Neill ignored them, turning a full 360 degrees,

searching through the maze of color. There—camouflaged by the mosaic floor—there was the control panel, off to one side of the Gate, in a little alcove, right where he would have expected to see it. He released a sigh of relief he hadn't even known he was holding. At least *something* had gone right on this mission, finally. There was a DHD here, even if it wasn't exactly pocket-size. The Serpent Guard standing by, apparently the Gate operator, waved acknowledgement and greeting to their escort. There was only one Guard at the console, and he was already half-hidden by the alcove. This might actually work. Now if he could only work out the details, like getting his hands on that bracelet, and getting rid of that inconvenient Guard . . .

The ambassador, who had led them through the Gate and then vanished on his own business, reappeared, having somehow managed to make the passage through the Gate without any sign of discomfiture. He looked over the huddle of Chosen and their wooden carts filled with primitive agrarian goods with an expression of weary disdain. He spoke, and the structure of the hall made his words into thunder.

"I am he who is called Nekhmet, servant of the Goa'uld. This is a place of the Great King, Apophis, Ruler of Worlds, Slayer of Enemies, He Who Is the Master of All, the Living One, Mighty One, Husband of the Great Royal Queen. You are his cattle. The fortunate among you will serve his servants and live forever. Enter into his palace and learn what it is to be the Chosen of the Goa'uld."

*Apophis.*

O'Neill could see the convulsion of hatred in Daniel's face and their eyes met, knowing, acknowledging. Neither one had speculated about the identities of the particular Goa'uld on the other end of the M'kwethet Gate. The fact that they were inimical to humanity was more than enough to know. Each knew what the other had suspected, and now it turned out to be true.

But that this was the actual home of Apophis, who had stolen Daniel Jackson's wife, Sha're, and Skaara, the boy Jack O'Neill had taken under his wing—to know that for certain—that was almost too much to bear.

Servant of the servants? O'Neill wondered whether they'd ever get within striking distance. He was a military man, a soldier, not an assassin. But for the chance to destroy Apophis, he might be willing to reconsider.

For Jackson there wasn't any indecision involved. O'Neill hoped the young scientist could hang on long enough for the colonel to get them both out of here.

Or rather, to get Carter and Teal'C, and then get them all home again.

"So that you will know the power of Apophis," the ambassador went on, "observe." He raised one hand, and the Chosen could clearly see the leather bracelet wrapped around the Jaffa's arm. Nekhmet raised his other hand and manipulated the round dial somehow.

The two Earth team members had seen Goa'uld technology, both mind-controlled and otherwise, used before, but even they were not prepared for what happened next.

From the bracelet came a flash of light, so bright the young people cried out, while the two older men shielded their eyes. They expected to see one or more of the Chosen lying dead when their vision readjusted.

Instead, they found themselves . . . elsewhere. The lotus-columned hall had disappeared, and instead of mosaic they found soft earth beneath their feet. The very scent of the air had changed, from dry dust to green growing things, trees and grass and butterflies that brushed against O'Neill's cheek and danced in the breeze before him. The walls around them were gone.

O'Neill whirled.

The control panel, with its arcane symbols, was gone. The Gate, too, was gone. All sign of human or alien habitation had vanished as if it had never been.

They were standing in the middle of an open field, bounded by tall trees. Blue mountains wreathed with clouds defined the horizon. A lake shimmered in bright sun. The breeze was just cool enough, the sun just warm enough. O'Neill had seen valleys like this in the Lakes district of upstate New York in summer, except that here there weren't any mosquitoes.

Valleys in upstate New York, however, didn't yet feature Serpent Guards or Egyptian-style courtiers, and the minions of the Goa'uld were still very much with them. Three of the Chosen fell to their knees before them.

"Where did it go?" Daniel asked, shaken. "How the hell did he do that?"

"I don't know," O'Neill answered grimly. "But we'd better hope he changes it back, because that's our only ticket out of here." He wished suddenly that Teal'C had come with him; the former Jaffa First would have known what was going on. Of course, he'd probably have been killed the moment the Serpent Guards laid eyes on him, too. "It doesn't feel like Chulak, anyway."

O'Neill took a deep breath and turned to look at the ambassador, only to find that Nekhmet was looking back at him, brows arched in unmistakable surprise. The colonel wasn't behaving anything like the kids, wasn't showing the panic and disorientation. Nekhmet was finally realizing, too, that two of his captives were considerably more mature than the rest. He signaled to the Jaffa, and O'Neill and Jackson found themselves separated from the rest, unsubtly urged over to the other man.

"Kneel before the servant of the Great One," one of the Jaffa suggested, dropping one end of his energy staff on O'Neill's shoulder. The blow to the strained muscle evoked a gasp, and O'Neill staggered.

Since he was going to his knees anyway, he decided to make the best of a bad situation and fell the rest of the way, catching himself with his hands. That aggravated his aching shoulders too, and he bit back an exclamation.

Out of the corner of his eye he could see Daniel dropping as well, bowing deeply and then sitting up, his hands clenching as he sat back on his heels. He carefully refrained from looking up at the man.

He was obviously a highly trusted Jaffa if he was allowed to use the bracelet, O'Neill thought rapidly. He was more than your average Jaffa, but obviously less than Apophis or any other Goa'uld. Another tiny piece of the puzzle that was the alien race.

"Who are you?" the ambassador demanded. "You are different from the others. Why?"

O'Neill was still trying to find the right words—a smart-aleck response wouldn't quite work in this situation—when Daniel spoke up. "We're here for the Great Ones," he said, his soft voice carrying conviction. "We seek Apophis, to give him the service he deserves of us."

*Oh, nicely done, Daniel,* O'Neill thought. The kid—well, he was a grown man, but O'Neill thought of him as a kid nonetheless—was one of the least convincing liars he'd ever met, but Daniel could tell the truth all day long and look you in the eye while he was doing it. It took a definite talent.

"Where are you from?"

"Where could we come from but M'kwethet?" Daniel bowed his head, breaking eye contact. "You have shown us a great wonder, and we fear you."

*Let's not lay it on too thick.* O'Neill could see the others out of the corner of his eye, staring at Jackson in amazement.

Nekhmet wasn't immune to shameless flattery. "It is but a taste of the power of the Goa'uld. Obey and serve, and you will see many more wonders, even greater than this."

"How could anything be greater?" Daniel asked, with just the right note of fear and insistent curiosity in his voice. "You have taken the place where we came from beneath our very feet, and now we're in some other place. How can this be? Where is the place that we were?"

O'Neill had eased himself back on his heels too, and was keeping his eyes cast down, listening hard, letting Daniel run the show for the moment. It was far more difficult for the colonel to play meek and diffident than it was for Jackson. Jackson had a streak of sheer iron in him, but he was at heart a far nicer person than O'Neill was.

Nekhmet was, unfortunately, not inclined to lay out all the answers in a convenient fashion.

"It is not your concern. Do not ask questions. Your place is to obey."

Daniel nodded, and then, gracefully, leaned forward and pressed his forehead to the earth at Nekhmet's feet. The little finger of his left hand tapped twice against the grass.

O'Neill could take a hint, but he didn't have to like it. He too leaned forward, though his gorge rose in protest against both the gesture and the vulnerability of the position. He rested his weight on the palms of his hands, and let the grass brush his face. It was petty, perhaps, but that was as far as he would go, even in pretense.

Nekhmet seemed satisfied and utterly unconscious that the two men before him had managed to avoid answering his questions. He stepped back and growled an order to the Serpent Guards in their own guttural language. The next thing O'Neill knew, he was being jabbed ungently in the kidneys as a signal that it was time to get up and get moving. He thought about rolling and bouncing to his feet, reviewed his various aches, cuts, and bruises, and reconsidered. He would save the dazzling surprise of his superb physical fitness for some other time, perhaps when he actually felt a bit more physically fit. But when he did, he promised himself, that particular Guard had a shock coming.

The kids were organizing themselves around the four tribute carts, picking up bundles that had fallen to the ground and piling them up again in a haphazard fashion. One of the wheels was askew on its spoke, and one of the kids had pointed it out. Several of them were now trying to raise the loaded cart up so that the wheel could be straightened and locked in place. Nekhmet observed with growing irritation.

"I wonder where all that stuff's going to go," Daniel observed quietly.

"I wonder why Nekky doesn't just wave his hand again," O'Neill retorted.

"Maybe the bracelet sent a code to some kind of transporter in the hall. Or he can only do that trick once."

"Once is one more than we needed."

The wheel was finally adjusted, more fallen bundles were replaced, and the group looked toward Nekhmet for guidance. He lifted his hand in an elegant fashion and pointed across the meadow to the trees. One of the Serpent Guards took point, while the rest deployed around the tribute.

"I guess we go over there," O'Neill remarked, as the two of them moved to join the little procession. As they moved off, he looked back over his shoulder to see if Nekhmet was going to soil his jeweled sandals by joining in the hike.

Apparently not. Where the ambassador had stood only moments before, there was only a blurring in the air, like heat distortion; then it, like the servant of the Goa'uld, was gone.

O'Neill amused himself by speculating about the military uses of possible interdimensional transport systems, while simultaneously studying the terrain. If this was the homeworld of the Goa'uld—the jury was still out on that one—it was a pleasant enough place. Judging by the number of flowers that had gone to seed, it was mid- to late summer.

Not too hot, not too cold. Very much like M'kwethet, in fact. The air was filled with vegetable perfumes.

Daniel was sneezing steadily.

O'Neill glanced over at the Serpent Guards, trudging along silently as escort. Once Nekhmet had disappeared, they seemed to feel free to let down their hair, or at least their helmets. One could be a cousin of Teal'C's—tall, massively muscled, ebony skin disfigured only by the golden cartouche of the Serpent embedded in his forehead. Like Teal'C, his face seemed carved of obsidian, the features immobile.

Two more of the Guards could have stepped off the beaches of California. O'Neill noted with interest the surfer tans; so the Guards didn't spend all their time in those helmets. He wondered where they were barracked, how they were trained. He made a note to ask Teal'C more about it when they got the team back together again.

The fourth Guard had the olive skin and dark, large liquid eyes of someone from the Indian subcontinent: Indian or Pakistani. O'Neill knew that none of these Guards had actually come from Earth, at least not in the sense of being born there, but their ancestors might very well have done so. Apparently Ra and his colleagues had picked over the whole planet looking for their slaves.

It was an interesting scrap of information, but not very useful. He could see Daniel coming to much the same conclusion, except that the archaeologist was probably planning a whole seminar series based on field interviews with the Jaffa on how much cultural drift had taken place between the stars. It was tough enough getting funding to keep the Gate open—he shuddered to think what Hammond's reaction to a grant proposal for anthropological research would be.

Eventually they worked their way through the trees, stopping every few feet to re-stack the carts when the vehicles tilted and toppled over tree roots. They came out of

the shade of the trees into bright sunlight again, and
shielded their eyes against the reflected dazzle of the
Goa'uld city.

The buildings were tall, square, and white, and seemed
bizarrely out of place in the green, soft valley. It took
O'Neill a moment or two to figure it out. The architecture
was reminiscent of pharaonic Egypt, recalling the desert
sands; it featured columns and heroic statues of seated
pharaohs and wide paved walkways.

But there were no desert sands here. Beside the walkways ran cheerful streams fringed with grass, and instead
of pyramids and sphinxes, the city was surrounded by
green mountains. It took another hour to get to the paved
road, where at least they could take advantage of the shade
of trees. They had plenty of time to study the buildings
as they approached. Once on the road, they were able to
move much more quickly, and soon were able to see more
details.

The white walls and the paved roads were made of large
square blocks, fitted together so closely that they could
barely see the lines between them. A thin trim of colored
squares, much like the colored mosaic of the Hall of the
Gate, defined the arched outlines of doors and windows.
The cobra helmets of the Guards flowed back into place,
and the four of them took up a more military position
around the tribute caravan.

"Wonder where we're going," Daniel muttered. A sheen
of sweat covered his fair skin, and the bridge of his nose
was beginning to redden. "I could use a drink of water."

"Likewise." They were proceeding between the buildings now, and O'Neill couldn't help but compare them
with the houses of M'kwethet. These buildings were
larger, more perfect somehow, showing no signs of normal erosion or wear and tear, as if the stone were a flaw-
less plastic replica of a natural material. Two of the Guards
had taken up position in front of them, with the other two

walking behind. The streets were empty, as if the city were empty of everything except themselves, Guards, and tribute.

"I wonder why the hike," Daniel went on.

"I think they're trying to impress us," O'Neill remarked. He was feeling the effects of the beating and the heat. "Okay, I'm impressed. Can we stop this now?"

"You okay?"

" 'Fine as frog hair,' as Hawkeye would say." He had to work at not panting as they walked, and his hand shook minutely as he wiped sweat out of his eyes. "Do frogs have hair?"

"I'm an archaeologist, not a biologist."

"Thank you, Dr. McCoy."

Turning a corner, they could see a broad avenue stretching perpendicular to their route. On one end was a massive temple, with rows of white columns at the top of a flight of shallow steps. The columns were crowned with lotus blossoms covered in glistening gold leaf.

On the other end of the avenue, perhaps half a mile away, facing the temple like an anxious supplicant, stood a smaller building, still at least three stories tall. Its columns were fewer, smaller, bare stone.

The arrangement was, in fact, very much like the relationship of the Gate to the Agora on M'kwethet. O'Neill wondered just how much of a coincidence that was supposed to be.

The Serpent Guards guided them to their left, to the smaller second building. The kids were showing their weariness, stumbling as they dragged the carts to the bottom of the tall, narrow steps. No ramps were visible.

"This building is *not* ADA-compliant," O'Neill said with great disgust. The kids looked at him with the same apprehension they might give any typical madman. Jackson rolled his eyes.

The Guards were not impressed. With quick, blunt gestures, they indicated that the carts were to be unloaded where they stood and the contents carried up the steps and into the building. Jackson and O'Neill stepped forward to help. Loading themselves with baskets of grain, they followed the Guards up the steps.

For the first time, other people appeared, taking the various packages and bundles. They were dressed in linen kilts, white triangular headscarves, plain gray broad metal collars, and leather sandals.

"Typical Old Kingdom servant dress," Jackson said, but even he blinked at the bare breasts of the woman who took the basket from him.

Once the carts were unloaded, Nekhmet came from the depths of the building and stood looking at them.

"This is the House of the Tribute," he said, "where you will make your home until you are Chosen of the Goa'uld or rejected to be returned to your world. You will find food here and places to sleep and work to do in the service of the Great Ones. You have been honored beyond all others of your world. Try to be worthy."

O'Neill snorted, but he did it softly. Nekhmet's outlined eyes didn't shift in his direction.

"You will be guided to your sleeping places by Ahmose, who is Overseer of the Tribute. Ahmose is my voice, as I am the Voice of Apophis."

"Where is this Apophis?" O'Neill spoke up.

Jackson groaned under his breath.

Nekhmet's finely arched brows climbed halfway up his forehead. "You will not question the ways of the Goa'uld," he said. "Most especially you will not question the ways of the Lord Apophis."

As he spoke, one of the Serpent Guards clubbed O'Neill down. Nekhmet strode forward to stare at the man writhing on the tiles before him. "You are insolent," he said. "Is this the kind of tribute M'kwethet sends us? It has been long since your world felt the discipline of the Goa'uld. Perhaps it is time again."

The others of the Tribute gasped.

O'Neill forced his eyes open, narrowed them to bring the two images of Nekhmet back into focus. "No," he forced himself to say. "M'kwethet . . . does not question . . . Apophis."

Jackson, on his knees beside him, bowed down. "We are the dust beneath the feet of the Goa'uld," he said rapidly. "We are your slaves, who seek only to discover how best to serve the magnificence of the Goa'uld. This man is nothing before you. Do not punish him for his eagerness to serve, I beg you."

"Perhaps if his tongue were removed he would not speak so intemperately," one of the Serpent Guards suggested.

"And he could not add his voice to the praises of Apophis. Surely the Great One does not wish his slaves mutilated unnecessarily? We are new to this world and this service. Allow us time to learn your ways, I entreat you."

Nekhmet appeared to consider the situation. He tilted his head, studying Jackson's groveling technique, and seemed well pleased.

"Very well," he said. "Ahmose will assign you your resting places. In time you will be summoned to service. Be sure that when that time comes you know proper behavior."

# CHAPTER TWELVE

The Council of the Rejected Ones of M'kwethet gathered in the remotest meeting room of the Agora, kicked off their sandals, and poured themselves a drink.

"Did we do the right thing?" Jareth asked.

Alizane spun a goblet between her fingers, lost in the play of light on the delicate glaze, and declined to answer.

"Yes," Karlanan rumbled. He was already on his second drink. "If we're lucky they were Selected right away and all we have to do is find the ones who are still here."

The dancing light on the glaze stood still as the goblet stopped moving.

"When I was Chosen," Karlanan went on, as if speaking to the walls, "I knew I was doing the right thing. That was the year of the rumors." He glared meaningfully at Alizane, who ignored him. "They told us nonsense about 'larvae' too, some of those who came back. I didn't believe them. I never saw such a thing. Did you? You were part of that tribute. Was it true?"

Alizane swallowed a deep draught and shook her head silently.

"Jareth? Did *you* ever see any?"

The older man stared at the floor. "I was a gardener," he apologized. "I spent all my time growing flowers and vegetables. The only larvae I ever saw were those of . . . insects."

"So." Karlanan finished his drink and poured himself a

third. "It *isn't* true. Never was." He nodded confidently to himself.

"Remind me," Alizane said suddenly. "How many Returned with you?"

There was a pause, as Karlanan considered. "Two," he said finally. "Me and Thos. Poor Thos," he went on thickly.

"Hanged himself, didn't he?" the woman said, an edge of malice in her voice.

"Yeah. Why'd he do that?" The youngest member of the Council finished his third drink, reached for the pitcher again, and reconsidered. "Doan' know why he did that."

"What happened to the rest?" Alizane asked, still studying her goblet.

Karlanan blinked. "The rest? Uh." Changing his mind, he filled his goblet again and drained it. "I dunno. Stayed, I guess."

"Why?" The question was gentle, insinuating, like a coiling snake.

"For the service of the Goa'uld and the honor of M'kwethet!" Karlanan tried to get to this feet and raise his cup in the toast, but staggered.

Jareth took the empty goblet away from him. "Time to go to bed, my friend," he suggested gently. "It's over now. It's all over."

"No, it isn't," the other man denied, peering at him owlishly. "Got to find those runaways. Got to punish them. They were s'posed to go. Didn't. 's not the honor of M'kwethet."

"That's all right," Jareth soothed. "Go on. Go home and rest. We'll deal with morning in the morning."

"Rather deal with it in the afternoon," Karlanan confided, giggling.

Jareth gave him a pained smile. "If you like. Go on, now."

Karlanan thought about it, finally nodded and staggered out the door.

Some minutes later, still staring at her goblet, Alizane said idly, "I suppose they've gone to the caves."

From behind her, sitting in a chair in the shadows against the wall, Jareth nodded. "Probably."

"Did you ever go there when you were young, Jareth? Did you ever daydream about fighting nobly against the Goa'uld?"

Jareth sighed. "I'm only a gardener, Alizane. There's nothing noble about a fighting gardener."

She snorted, a half-strangled laugh. "You were a gardener. I cleaned latrines in the Serpent Guard barracks. Surely that prepares us well to govern our people."

"Who else would do it?" Jareth asked. "At least we *know*."

Alizane took a deep breath and put her goblet down. "Do we? Does Karlanan? How much have we forgotten because we can't bear to remember?"

"When I need to remember," Jareth said, "I go to the Spoiled City on the other side of the mountains, and it reminds me of everything I need to know. We *are* doing the right thing, Alizane."

She closed her eyes and swallowed. "I hope so."

"And tomorrow or the next day we can go up to the caves and bring the youngsters home. We don't have to tell Karlanan. We can outvote him, after all." He got to his feet and held out a hand to her. "It will all pass, and our people will remain at peace. Come, my dear. It's time to go home."

By the time Samantha Carter climbed the last steep slope up to the cave, it was nearly dark. So when Teal'C silently materialized out of the shadows, she gasped and went for her sidearm. Fortunately for them both, the Jaffa merely stood, waiting for her to recognize him. He chose to ignore her abashed reholstering of her weapon and waited politely for her to regain her composure before asking, pointedly, "Where are O'Neill and Jackson?"

She swallowed hard and checked to make sure their little band of refugees were all safely out of earshot before responding. "They're gone," she said. "They went through the Gate with the Chosen ones. The colonel said to wait until after they were gone and then bring the kids back."

"You spoke to him?"

"Not exactly." The whole story of how she'd received her orders could wait, she decided. She'd occupied the hours climbing back to their refuge with equal parts of dodging search parties and thinking hard. "There must be some way to open the Gate from this side; if they go with the tribute they can find out how to do it, and come back for us, and then we can all get back home."

Teal'C nodded approval. "It is a good plan. But it requires them to place themselves at the mercy of the Goa'uld."

"And the Goa'uld haven't got any." Carter finished the thought for him, shuddering. "But the orders were clear: We have to get the kids together—the rest of the kids—and go back to the M'kwethet Gate and wait for 'developments.'"

Elsewhere, on a world far, far away, Daniel Jackson sat cross-legged on a stone floor, meditating. Across the room from him, Jack O'Neill lay on a cot, snoring.

It was a big room, relatively speaking, at least fifteen by fifteen feet. Jackson suspected that under normal circumstances it would provide sleeping quarters for at least six, instead of the two Earth team members. Ahmose had decided, quite rightly, to isolate the possible source of trouble by putting them together and far away from the already-cowed younger members of the tribute.

They had stored all the goods away, each in its own dedicated room, with a significant part set aside for shipment elsewhere. Jackson had been fascinated to see the feather room, filled to overflowing with plumes of every size, color, and description. Unfortunately, the dust they accumulated had sent him into a sneezing fit that almost brought him to his knees. Part of his mind was still busily developing hypotheses about what possible use a highly technological race like the Goa'uld would have for feathers. Ceremonial purposes, no doubt.

The Goa'uld were very ceremonial. They'd adopted wholesale, or possibly even influenced, many of Earth's mythologies, especially those of ancient Egypt. He was more inclined to the former theory, given the unbelievable mishmash of customs, artifacts, and attire they exhibited; it was as if they had sampled Egyptian culture at irregular intervals from the predynastic period clear up through the Roman conquest, and picked whatever they liked best whether it all fit together or not. Ahmose, for instance— that was the name of a pharaoh. Was it likely that a slave would share a royal name? Maybe. Maybe not.

Apophis. The enemy of Ra, the Great Serpent who attempted to devour the Sun God's boat when he finished his daily journey across the skies. He wondered if the rivalry between the Egyptian deities was reflected in Goa'uld politics. He wondered if the Goa'uld actually had politics.

No, wait. Of course they did. There was Ra, who was Apophis's rival. Jackson didn't think the Goa'uld had adopted the name by accident. Apophis might swear vengeance against Earth for destroying Ra, but that didn't mean he wouldn't have done it himself if he'd had the chance. Then there was Nekhmet, subordinate to Apophis. Hierarchies. Rivalries. Jealousies?

Apophis. Sighing, he pressed the heels of his hands against his eyes, unable to press away the cold worm of hatred at the thought of that name. He was unable, too, to press away the inevitable thought that accompanied it.

Where Apophis was, Sha're would be. His love, his joy, his life. His stolen wife, implanted with a mature Goa'uld. Somewhere on this world was Sha're, and chance had given him one more tantalizing opportunity to find her.

O'Neill rolled over, snuffling into the hard pillow, and Jackson smiled fleetingly. The colonel hated to admit not being at his absolute best at all times, but he'd headed for that cot as if it were a long-lost friend. It was a good thing the Council of M'kwethet wasn't a better judge of character; they'd picked the wrong captive to torture. Although, O'Neill had remarked, it did present an interesting variation—good prisoner/bad prisoner—it just showed that the M'kwethet grasp of the whole "ruthless brutality" concept was a bit slippery.

There were worse attributes to be known for.

Jackson sighed. No matter how much he tried to empty his mind, to free himself from the underlying panic and hatred that ate at him, the image of Apophis and Sha're would not go away.

All right, then; what could he do about it?

O'Neill's goal was to reunite the team and get them home. In order to do that, they had to locate the bracelet Nekhmet used, or one just like it; figure out how to use it; retrieve the two left on M'kwethet; and get home again, all without alerting the Guards or the Goa'uld.

What if he could find Sha're and bring her back too? Of course, there was always the little problem of the Goa'uld parasite, but they could deal with that somehow.

That they were prisoners under the supervision of Ahmose and Nekhmet was another irrelevant detail.

Surely he could convince O'Neill that they could combine the necessary search for the Gate with his own search for Sha're? And if they found her, they'd probably find Skaara too.

At this point Jackson took a deep breath and shook his head. He knew Jack O'Neill. The colonel would be tempted, even sympathetic, but he wouldn't buy the argument for one minute, not if it threatened his primary objective, to save his team. If Jackson was going to try this, he'd have to do it on his own.

Mumbling came from the bed across the room.

Through a little square window high up on the wall, he could see the sky fading to purple and rose as the sun set. Giving up on the meditation idea, he got up and looked around the room for lamps, candles, some source of light. Nothing was immediately apparent.

The Goa'uld had their own mysterious methods of lighting.

Then again, they might not waste those methods on mere cattle.

"Going somewhere?" came a voice from the bed.

"Uh . . . " Jackson stammered. "I was looking for some light."

"Mmmph." O'Neill sat up, a little less smoothly than was his wont, and groaned. "Oh, man." He rotated his head, slowly, and Jackson could hear his spine cracking from across the room. "I'd guess it's after curfew anyway."

"The sun just set."

"Whatever." The colonel got up, slapped imaginary dust off his pants, and stretched. The white robe of the Chosen was a discarded heap upon the floor. "I don't suppose there's facilities around here?"

"Over there." Hygiene seemed to have followed the model on M'kwethet, or more likely vice-versa. In any case, there was a screen at one end of the room. O'Neill disappeared behind it for a few minutes and then came out again, drying his hands on the white robe from the floor.

"Food?"

Jackson shook his head.

"I don't suppose we could raid the kitchen?"

Jackson shrugged. "I don't know if there is a kitchen."

"Think positive." O'Neill looked down at the robe in his hands and dropped it on the floor again, went to his belt and pulled out a white T-shirt. Even in the fading light Jackson could see the bruises on the other man's ribs and jaw. "Well, what are you waiting for? Let's go scout up some breakfast. Or dinner. Or something."

"Wouldn't the door be—"

As Jackson spoke, the unlocked door swung open at O'Neill's push. "It's a barracks, not a prison," he said. "They've probably got guards all over the place, sensors, the whole works, but they don't need to lock us up. Where would we go?"

*Good question*, Jackson thought grimly, as he trailed the other man down the plain stuccoed hallway. The passage was lighted, though he couldn't find the source of the illumination.

Sure enough, as soon as they came to a corner they saw one of the Jaffa standing guard. He was engaged in bantering conversation with a dark-haired young woman who balanced a basket on one hip. Both conversants looked up as the two men approached.

"Hi," O'Neill said cheerfully. "We're new around here. Is there someplace we can get something to eat?"

The Jaffa straightened, frowning, but the woman laughed. She had shockingly bright blue eyes, vivid against a Mediterranean complexion. Jackson blinked; laughter wasn't a sound he had ever associated with a Goa'uld world. Nor was that particular eye color. And she had no cartouche mark on her forehead.

"You must be part of that shipment that came in earlier today," she said. "Ahmose said that some of you would be sent to your quarters right away, but I don't think he meant to starve you! The evening meal is done, but come with me. I'll see that you get something."

The Jaffa opened his mouth, perhaps to protest.

"Ah, be still," the woman rebuked him. "No one goes

hungry in my house. I am Mafret," she added to the two team members. "I am the housekeeper for my lord Ahmose. Come with me to the kitchens."

"I'm Jack," O'Neill smiled down at her. She barely came to his shoulder. Her hair was a glossy blue-black, and she wore a thin, unbleached linen tunic that came to her ankles and tied over one shoulder. "He's Daniel. He's shy."

Jackson glared at him. O'Neill smiled beatifically.

Mafret raised the basket and settled it on her head, steadying it with one graceful hand, and led the way, hips swaying. O'Neill gave Jackson a wide-eyed *Well, what would* you *do?* look and followed, leaving a discomfited Jaffa guard behind.

The housekeeper led them down the hall and around the corner, down a series of steps and down another hall. Jackson was beginning to get thoroughly lost. It was a larger building than he had thought, easily large enough to house two or three hundred people. If Mafret was the housekeeper in charge of all this, plus the staff it would take to keep that many people fed, clothed, and clean, she had a great deal of responsibility indeed.

As they walked, they passed a number of people, all of whom recognized Mafret and acknowledged her, either by nods or bows or, in the case of the many carrying burdens on their heads, by a casting down of the eyes. She returned every greeting, often by name, but didn't introduce her two charges.

Eventually they came to a large kitchen. At least, Jackson assumed it was a kitchen; he couldn't see a fireplace or a stove anywhere. But there were huge clay jars stained about the rims with oil, and baskets big enough to hide a man if they hadn't been filled to overflowing with grain; loosely woven wicker and wire baskets hanging from bare rafters held vegetables, some of which he recognized as onions, potatoes, jicama. The walls were lined with doors.

Besides, the place smelled like a kitchen, like baking and stew and pastries. Two girls, dressed in the same kind of sheer linen tunic, scrubbed flour dust off a broad stone table. Mafret swayed over to one wall and set her burden down on the floor, shaking her head briskly.

"Well, then," she said. "I suppose my lord gave you no instruction at all about your life here and what is expected of you?"

"No, ma'am." O'Neill was laying it on a bit too thick, Jackson thought disapprovingly. That ingratiating grin was beginning to get on his nerves. "Maybe you could help us out?"

The girls giggled. Apparently they thought so too.

Mafret seemed to share their opinion. She gave O'Neill a long, comprehensive look. "What I can do is feed you and clothe you properly." She snapped orders to the girls in a quick, fluid dialect that Jackson didn't follow, and the two scurried away, still looking over their shoulders and giggling. As soon as they were gone, the housekeeper set about assembling a meal, opening doors and collecting utensils, plates, drinking mugs, and finally, from a door that looked exactly like the rest, a heavy bowl of stew and several small loaves of steaming, warm bread.

Jackson was hungrier than he thought. He barely waited for the arched-eyebrow permission to start digging in, and then had to stop almost immediately—the bowl that the woman had handled with her bare hands was filled with excruciatingly hot food. O'Neill, watching him, took it a little slower, but even he was surprised.

The vegetables might not be corn, beans, and squash, but they tasted good and were filling. They finished their servings and asked for more.

Mafret watched them eat with considerable satisfaction. As they started on second helpings, the two girls came in with armfuls of clothing. Mafret directed them to set the clothing on one of the tables and then chased them away.

"This is terrific," O'Neill said at last. "Thank you."

Mafret gave him a puzzled smile. "Why do you thank me? This is my purpose."

O'Neill let go a resigned breath. "Then you fulfill your purpose very, very well, ma'am. We do appreciate your taking the trouble to feed us."

"Absolutely," Jackson chimed in belatedly. He was still having trouble chewing around the burns in his mouth, but somehow he managed.

O'Neill watched as Mafret refilled his mug for the fourth time, and then picked idly at the remains of the third loaf of bread. "Mafret," he said abruptly, "where are we?"

She looked at him sharply, then at Jackson, and seated herself across the table from the two of them. "You do not know?"

"We know we were on M'kwethet," O'Neill said. "And we went through a Gate and found ourselves in a big room with a blue tile floor and paintings on the walls. And then suddenly we were in a meadow. And now we're here. Where is here?"

"Saqqara, of course."

Jackson was unable to stifle a laugh, and regretted it immediately as Mafret focused a hurt blue gaze on him. O'Neill waited for enlightenment.

"Saqqara's the site of some of the first known Egyptian tombs," he explained. "Like Abydos."

"So this place belonged to Ra as well?"

Mafret immediately became agitated. "You must not speak the name of the Great One who is gone," she said, glancing over her shoulder. "The Goa'uld will punish you."

"Ra is dead," O'Neill said deliberately. "How can he hurt us?"

"There are other Great Ones."

"Like Apophis."

Mafret went white. "Be still. Have you no sense? There are Jaffa everywhere."

The pretense of flirting evaporated. "You aren't Jaffa," O'Neill said, leaning across the table to her.

She shuddered. "That is not my fate, and I thank the gods for it. I am a servant and beneath their notice, and would stay so."

O'Neill nodded. "All right, then. Tell us about this house. What is it?"

She swallowed and sat back. "This is the servant house of the lord Ahmose, who serves Nekhmet, who serves the Great One. We are privileged to provide food and body servants to the court of the Great One."

"How many people you got here?" The loaf of bread was no more than a pile of crumbs now.

Mafret paused a moment, her lips moving silently. "Three hundred and sixty-six souls sleep in the servant house of my lord," she said at last. "Including you."

"Three hundred and sixty-six?" Daniel repeated, shocked. "How many Goa'—I mean, how many Great Ones are there?"

Mafret shrugged. "I don't know. This house serves the house of the one Great One."

"Apophis." O'Neill supplied the name for her. She flinched, but nodded silent, emphatic agreement.

"Are there servant houses for each of the Great Ones?" Daniel asked, his mind reeling at the idea. Three hundred and sixty-six . . . *Don't be ridiculous*, he scolded himself. Any of the European courts had more servants than that on their worst day.

But the European courts didn't invade their servants, destroy their minds and personalities . . .

*You sure about that?*

At that point Daniel decided his inner voice had been hanging out with O'Neill too long.

Mafret, oblivious to the inner dialogue, was shaking her

head again. "I don't know. My duty is this house and no other."

O'Neill sighed, then caught his breath as a rib jabbed. Mafret got up immediately and went over to another of the featureless doors, rummaged behind it for a few moments, and came out again with a folded packet of powder about the size of a tea bag. She poured the contents into O'Neill's cup and presented it to him. "Drink."

"Uh—what is that?"

Mafret wasn't used to having her authority questioned, at least not on housekeeping issues. Physical pain was evidently a housekeeping issue. "Drink!" she snapped.

O'Neill shrugged, winced again, and drank obediently, making a face as he did so. "All right. Yeech." Noticing Mafret's stern expression, he made an apologetic gesture.

"The Gate we came through, " he continued, pushing the mug to one side. "Where is that?"

Mafret checked to make sure the mug was empty. "It is in the House of the Great One, of course."

"So they took us to his house and then bounced us out of town?" Daniel asked. "Why?"

"To show you their power," she said matter-of-factly. Since they were finished eating, she gathered up the utensils and took them over to place them in a drawer, pressing one corner as she shut it. Daniel thought he heard a hum coming from the drawer. "They do not do so often, but sometimes those who come here are very foolish."

"Really?" O'Neill said with a wolflike grin. "How foolish are they?"

She looked down at him, a slender waiflike figure with old, old eyes. Cleopatra, Daniel realized abruptly. She reminded him of a younger version of Elizabeth Taylor as Cleopatra, with those enormous violet eyes and the glossy black hair.

"Sometimes," she said deliberately, "there are those who think that they can use the Gate to escape the Great

Ones. Or they think the Great Ones can be harmed. Those who think this are very foolish, and they always die. They take a very long time dying."

"But others come and always try, don't they?" O'Neill said softly, the look of the wolf still in his eyes.

"Yes," Mafret admitted reluctantly. "But only because they don't know how useless it is. There are the ones who have not been told, and then there are the stupid ones who have been told and don't believe."

O'Neill smiled, acknowledging. "So only an ignorant or a stupid man could ever succeed."

Her lips curved as she smiled back despite herself. "Even so." Her hair swept back and forth as she shook her head abruptly, as if shaking off a spell. "If you try you will fail. No one succeeds.

"Besides," she went on, as another thought occurred to her, "are you not sacrifices from M'kwethet? Those from M'kwethet come willingly. Why would you want to leave, now that you're here?"

The sublime logic of this was unanswerable. O'Neill tried—at least, his jaw dropped—but he was unable to come up with a response.

"Mafret," Daniel stepped in, "have you ever wanted to be possessed by a Goa'uld?"

The look of loathing she gave him was answer enough.

"Well," he said, "we feel the same way. And don't tell anybody, but we're not really from M'kwethet. We'd like to get back home, in fact, but we have a couple of things we have to do first. So you see it's important for us to know some things.

"Like that bracelet of Nekhmet's. It can open a Gate, can't it? We need to find it. Soon."

"As soon as possible, in fact," O'Neill put in.

Mafret stared from one to the other. "I see," she said slowly. "You want me to help you find a Jaffa's Key and escape from Saqqara."

"Exactly," O'Neill said, with a winning smile.

Daniel's heart sank.

Sure enough, Mafret laughed at them.

Rising from the table, she shook her head. "Go back to your room and sleep," she said with a kind of fondness. "Tomorrow you'll be called out by Ahmose and given your first duties in service of the Great Ones. You need to be rested for it."

"You're not going to help us," O'Neill clarified.

"Of course I'm not going to help you," she snapped, finally letting exasperation show. "Am I a fool? No. I am the housekeeper of the servant house. If you wish to find a Key, or to leave this world, you will do it without help from me."

O'Neill studied her for a long moment. "And without hindrance?" he asked softly.

She stared back, for a long, silent moment. Then, finally, she said, "I keep this house. What occurs outside of it is not my concern."

"Good enough," the colonel replied. He paused once more. "So you never go out of this house? How long have you served the Goa'uld, Mafret?"

She raised her head with pride, the indirect lighting glistening in her hair. "I have served *Ahmose* since my birth," she said. "He is my father. It is right that I should do so."

"You serve the Goa'uld," O'Neill said flatly. "Whether you say so or not. And you know what they are."

Mafret stepped back from the table, as if creating more than physical distance between herself and O'Neill's words. "Go back to your room," she snapped, "before I call the Jaffa to discipline you."

O'Neill rose to his feet and looked down at her. "I'd like to assume you just don't know any better," he said, his voice still soft. "But I think you do. And that makes you even worse than they are."

She opened her mouth to make outraged protest, and he raised one hand to forestall her. "Oh, we'll go."

Daniel stood up hastily behind him.

"But you know the truth, Mafret, and you know that being the daughter of Ahmose won't be enough to save you if Apophis decides to take you. So you make sure you stay safe, and never go outside. Because the monster's gonna get you otherwise."

The two of them left her staring after them.

# CHAPTER THIRTEEN

Samantha Carter knelt beside the pallet, her hands on her thighs, and wished she'd studied medicine instead of astrophysics.

Before her lay Maesen, her brown hair fanned out on the coarse woven pillow. Her breath whistled in and out of her lungs, every breath bubbling loudly enough to be heard across the cavern. Her eyes were half open, staring at nothing.

Clein'dori knelt gracefully beside her, the glass in her hand half full of a thick green liquid. "Here," she said, sliding an arm underneath her friend's head and shoulders. "Mae—drink this—"

The lifting action resulted in a distinct sloshing sound from the girl's lungs and a spate of weak coughing and gagging. Maesen resisted ineffectually. When Clein'dori allowed her to lie back again, the sick girl's lips were rimmed with green.

"What is that?" Carter asked softly.

"I found a saying in the chests by the wall," she said, equally softly. "It spoke of plants and mixtures to be used for sickness." She sat up and brushed long blond hair back over her shoulder. "We haven't needed such things for a long time."

"Because the Goa'uld cured all your diseases."

Clein'dori nodded, her blue-gray eyes remote. "We've never had sickness until you came."

The unspoken accusation hung in the air between the two women.

"On our world," Carter said, feeling as if she were making excuses, "this is a little sickness. We have so many, we fight them off and become strong so that a little cold is nothing."

Clein'dori let loose a little sigh. "Perhaps that's why you're so eager to fight the Goa'uld," she said, smoothing Maesen's hair away from her sweat-slicked forehead. "You spend all your time fighting. You even fight sickness."

"If we don't fight, we die."

"Whereas we do not fight. And until now, our people lived."

Carter closed her eyes. "Are you sorry you came with us?"

Behind them, Teal'C and the boys crouched over a small fire, cooking something that smelled of roasted meat. Markhtin had thrown off the infection fairly quickly, though he still had a runny nose. Maesen, though, had gotten steadily and rapidly worse. Now, even though Carter didn't want to admit it, she was dying, drowning in the fluids accumulated in her lungs.

Clein'dori set the cup aside, catching it as it tilted against a pebble and threatened to spill the remains of the rough medicine.

"No," she said at last. "I've seen the thing that lives inside of your friend Teal'C, and it frightens me. What he has told us of how the thing grows, how it takes over human beings, frightens me. It frightens me more that even if I were Rejected and came back to my home, I might have a child one day that would be used so. So, no, I'm not sorry. And I'll keep my children from the selection as well.

"But I wonder how many of my friends will die for my selfishness."

"You could wonder too how many will live, in the long run, along with your children."

Maesen coughed again, gagging. A line of green mucus trailed out of the corner of her mouth.

Clein'dori wiped it gently away. "I do wonder," she murmured. "I do."

On their way back to their room through the labyrinth of halls, Jackson and O'Neill caught sight of one of the Jaffa guards, following at a fairly discreet distance and making no effort to hide himself. They carried with them the clothing Mafret had provided: the same tunics everyone else wore, a matching set of plain gray metal collars, and something they finally decided must be underwear.

The Jaffa kept following, sometimes no more than a dozen paces behind.

If nothing else, it provided an incentive to find the right path back without doing too much hesitating at the intersections. Fortunately, O'Neill had a good memory; he wasn't the type to ask for directions, particularly of a Goa'uld slave. When they had regained their room and closed the door behind them, they could distinctly hear the "thud" of an energy staff grounded in parade rest.

"Get the feeling Mafret doesn't trust us?" O'Neill asked ironically.

"Would you?"

O'Neill grinned without humor. "Nope. Not as far as I could throw us. But I'd do a little better job of restraining my prisoners. Looks like these folks don't get too many escape attempts."

"Yeah." Jackson was tired, suddenly. They were going to break out, he knew it, and if they were lucky they would even make it back to M'kwethet. Right back where they started. And Sha're was just as far away as ever. "Maybe they think we're going to restrain ourselves."

It was a lame attempt at a joke, and O'Neill didn't even bother to acknowledge it. He was standing on the bed beneath the window, lifting himself up to peer outside. "I

don't know what that stuff was she gave me," he remarked
as an aside, "but it works pretty good. Maybe we should
try to get hold of some to take back with us." After some
struggling, he managed to get his head and one arm
through the opening.

"Are you planning to go out that window?" Jackson
asked when the other man's efforts abruptly stopped.

O'Neill slid back inside. "Uh, no. Looks like it's about
six stories straight down."

"I thought we were on the ground floor!"

"I think the ground kinda tilts." For a moment O'Neill
looked nonplussed. "We could try to get past Alphonse."

"And go where, exactly? And how many alarms will we
set off in the process? Don't we need some idea where
we're going first?"

"You know, Daniel, there are times I don't like you
much . . . got any better ideas?"

Jackson settled cross-legged on one of the other beds.
"Yes, as a matter of fact. If this city is built on the model
of many ancient Earth cities, then that wide avenue runs
down the center, and we're at one end and the other important buildings are at the other. I'm betting that big building
we saw is the one where the Gate is. It's probably where
Nekhmet lives, too." *Where Sha're is.* "Let's take the
opportunity to rest tonight. If Ahmose is going to give us
our 'duties' tomorrow, we may be able to get there without
killing anybody along the way."

"Unless Mafret tells him otherwise."

Jackson shrugged. "That's the chance we take. Meanwhile, I'm tired."

"I'm not."

"I can't imagine why."

"Daniel, are you getting sarcastic in your old age?"

Jackson shrugged and smiled.

O'Neill drew a deep breath. "Okay. We probably won't

have time to discuss this in any more detail later, so let's review the plan:

"We have to find the bracelet—what Mafret called the Jaffa's Key. And we have to figure out how to use it. Once we do that, we open the Gate and go back to M'kwethet to get Carter and Teal'C, and then hop back to Earth."

Daniel swallowed. O'Neill had given him some idea of what he was planning back on M'kwethet, and it had sounded insane at the time. Now there was no way to pretend that the other man could actually pull off a miracle. "There's no way we can activate that Gate without anybody noticing. There's the guard, or operator. And there were other people in that room."

O'Neill let go a long breath. "I know that. But *we're going to get away with it* because this is the only chance we've got.

"First we have to find a Key. If we get really lucky, we can replace that console operator and nobody will notice. I'm betting there's a lot of traffic that goes through there, but there's quiet times too. We'll work our trip in with all the other traffic going through. Make it look like just business as usual."

"What if they catch us at it, and can tell where we've gone? They'll send troops after us."

O'Neill smiled. "We'll cross that bridge when we come to it, shall we?" He didn't point out that if something like that happened, it would mean they were likely already dead. Daniel decided he was grateful for the discretion. "Maybe you'll just have to make like the Marx brothers and lead them in circles for a while. But we're going to take the first available opportunity, Daniel, so be ready."

O'Neill sounded confident—but he always sounded confident. It was part of being a leader, part of inspiring the troops. But Jackson wasn't a troop.

He was a scientist, and the theory behind this attempt was so full of holes it made his head spin. Carter and

Teal'C probably had a much better chance of survival if they stayed exactly where they were for the rest of their natural lives.

But O'Neill's job was to get them home, even if the road led right into hell, or Apophis's front hall.

Which, in fact, it did.

"What about the transport trick Nekhmet used?" he asked, in a last-ditch effort to restore some rationality to the conversation. "What if we find ourselves back in that meadow?"

O'Neill closed his eyes briefly, and Jackson realized suddenly how very tired the other man really was, even after his long nap followed by a night's uninterrupted sleep. "I'm betting they won't pull that stunt around either the console or the Gate," he said at last. "Nekhmet waited until we were well away before he did it, and all the supplies came with us. They wouldn't want to toss their Gate or DHD around. The trick may even be keyed to that particular part of the floor."

"So he really didn't do it at all. It was mechanical." For some reason, that disappointed Jackson; it was a lot easier to resign himself to battling a race that was omnipotent. If they weren't, it meant he and O'Neill really did have to follow through and try this madness, because they might actually get away with it.

And if they didn't get away with it, it would probably be his fault.

"Get some rest, Daniel," O'Neill advised. "Big day on the slave block tomorrow."

The next morning they were awakened by relentless pounding on their door, followed by Jaffa with energy staffs prodding them to their feet. Jackson overheard O'Neill muttering something about boot camp, but he didn't have the time or inclination to ask questions as they were herded out the door and down the hall. They barely had time to pull on their clothing, and spent the trip down the hall trying to figure out how to put on their collars. Others, similarly rousted out, joined them in a steadily widening stream of humanity.

The one time Jackson hung back he saw, out of the corner of his eye, an energy staff rise and fall, and heard a stifled cry. O'Neill had seen the same thing. Both of them picked up their pace. Along the way they picked up the rest of the tribute group. O'Neill had been ready to throw his collar away when he noticed that everyone in the group except the tribute from M'kwethet was wearing them. It seemed to distinguish between the newcomers and the old-timers. He decided instantly that he blended in better as an old-timer.

They found themselves herded into a room large enough to hold seven or eight times their number. The others from M'kwethet clumped together for security's sake, and whispered among themselves. The room continued to fill with others, also dressed in the plain kilts, tunics, and head-cloths of the human slaves, who looked at the newcomers with mild curiosity.

Their attention was rudely yanked away by the entrance of Ahmose, followed by his daughter and a couple of Jaffa guards. It wasn't entirely clear whether the Jaffa served as escort or whether Ahmose, too, was in custody. Still, the sight of the Jaffa was more than enough to silence the crowd.

"Welcome to the service of the Great Ones," Ahmose announced, his voice pitched high in an effort to carry to the back of his audience. Evidently he wasn't in custody after all. The fact that he rated a Jaffa escort, then, surely meant he must be fairly important. "Those of you who are new to this service will receive today the first of your duties. You will carry them out excellently, without question, without complaint, and you will prosper. Fail to do so, and you will die."

The newcomers murmured wordlessly. Jackson found himself stretching to see over the people in front of him. He'd managed to snatch up his glasses on the way, but now had to take them off to polish away a smudge. One of these days he was going to get surgery or something, he promised himself, so he wouldn't be so damned helpless. One of these days. He felt in his belt for the reassuring cool metal of the signaler. Still there, thank God.

Vision-enabled once more, he stretched again. Yes, that blur focused now into Mafret, standing demurely behind Ahmose with her hands folded prayerlike in front of herself. She looked nothing like her father, Jackson thought, and a good thing too, considering that Ahmose was almost certainly bald beneath the skullcap he wore.

O'Neill had drifted away, closer to the front of the crowd.

Mafret stepped forward.

"This is Mafret. You will obey her words as you obey mine."

Bowing, Mafret gave her father a tightly rolled scroll. He made a production out of untying it, removing caps from either end, and opening it, stretching a length of thick white paper. It looked like actual papyrus, Jackson thought.

"This is the command of the Great One."

At the words, the audience began to go to their knees. Those who were slower found themselves encouraged by blows from the Jaffa, who were now moving among them. Jackson, who had more or less expected the reaction, was already on his way down. O'Neill waited until the very last moment, engaging in a staring match with Mafret all the while. Her face was impassive as he finally went to his knees. O'Neill was spending a lot of time on this mission trying to stare down women, Jackson thought.

Ahmose looked over the kneeling assembly with almost as much satisfaction as if they were actually kneeling to him. "Even so shall you greet the commands of the Great Ones. Never shall you look up to them, for their gaze is death to mortal kind."

Their eyes glowed, true, Jackson acknowledged silently. But the death came from the ribboned hand weapons they wore.

He wondered how many of those in the room were tribute from other worlds like M'kwethet and how many had been born here on Saqqara. Some had probably been kidnapped by force from other worlds, too. But everyone here seemed to know generally what was going on, which argued that Saqqara might be a special case.

"Thus say the Great Ones: Some among you will come to the House of the Great Ones, and some will go forth to labor in the fields and mines. In all things you will serve the Great Ones."

Jackson was getting pretty sick of hearing the Goa'uld referred to as "Great Ones." He could only imagine what O'Neill must think about it.

In fact, O'Neill wasn't thinking about merc nomenclature at all. He was paying careful attention to Mafret, whose gaze still strayed from time to time in his direction. If she kept it up, one of the Jaffa was going to notice, and that was never a good thing.

"Here you will be taught your duties by Mafret. Heed her—"

A gasp rippled through the tightly packed crowd, originating from the back of the room. Several of those kneeling were sent sprawling as a double line of Serpent Guards in full regalia, red cobra eyes glowing, marched into the room and forced a corridor from the door to the trembling Ahmose. Between the Guards came Nekhmet.

As Nekhmet entered, Ahmose and Mafret too went to their knees, and a moan of terror rose from the crowd. In seconds, what had appeared to be an impressive dignitary, giving advice and instruction to the uninitiated, was reduced to the same level as the rest of them: mere human slave.

"Ahmose!"

The pudgy little man whimpered. When the silence stretched out, he began to crawl forward on his belly, his face pressed to the floor. O'Neill managed to tilt his head to one side enough to see Mafret shrink back against the wall as her father crept to the Jaffa's sandaled feet and began to kiss the floor before them. A glance upward confirmed that Nekhmet was wearing the bracelet still. It was probably a badge of his authority when it wasn't opening Gates.

Had Teal'C had a Key? He'd never mentioned one. Maybe it was something new. Maybe only a very few of the Jaffa were permitted to use portable DHDs. There was no telling.

But if there were only a few, his target conveniently narrowed itself directly to the man in front of him.

Nekhmet stared down at Ahmose, a little smile playing about his face. Finally he repeated, almost tenderly, "Ahmose. Rise."

Ahmose came to his knees, his head still bowed, his chin still pressed to his chest.

"I seek the tribute from M'kwethet," Nekhmet informed him. From the other side of the room, not far from where Daniel Jackson crouched, came an involuntary cry. The smile broadened. "You will send them all to the house of my lord for his pleasure. I would show my lord, when he comes, the manner of tribute that M'kwethet sends him— its aged and halt, instead of the young and strong."

O'Neill sucked in a breath. "Aged and halt" could only refer to himself and Daniel. And "the house of my lord"— if Daniel was right, that meant they were going to be sent directly to the building where they had arrived, the building that housed Apophis. If the Goa'uld lord saw them, he would certainly recognize them from several unpleasant encounters in the past. And Apophis would try to obtain the transmitter that unlocked the iris protecting the Earth Gate.

On the upside, they were also going to be sent directly to the building that housed the Saqqara Stargate.

All in all, it would probably save them considerable sneaking-around time—if they could stay alive that long.

Across the room, similar thoughts were running through Daniel Jackson's mind, with one essential difference. He didn't think of it as being sent into the proximity of the Gate.

He thought of it as getting much, much closer to the potential presence of Sha're.

# CHAPTER FOURTEEN

O'Neill's eyes met Mafret's across the room. He wasn't quite sure whether he was asking for help, or what kind of help the diminutive housekeeper could offer, or what opportunity there might be.

She caught his look and lifted her chin, a red flush spreading over her cheekbones, and then she swallowed abruptly and signaled to one of the men nearby.

He stepped forward in turn and crouching, touched Ahmose on the shoulder. Ahmose scuttled backward before getting to his feet. Nekhmet, sublimely confident that his merest wish would be followed, had already turned away.

Ahmose had a rapid exchange of words with the man, and then Mafret came up and added something. Ahmose nodded. The servant stepped forward, clearing his throat.

"All those who are of the tribute of M'kwethet shall present themselves, as has been ordered by the Lord Nekhmet. Those who serve in the kitchen of the Great House, in the yards of the Great House, and in the inner chambers thereof shall also prepare and present themselves for their daily tasks, and be quick in service to the Great One!"

That brought a few yelps of dismay, as the non-tribute slaves were caught off guard by their summons. There was considerable confusion and milling around as some dashed out to warn their coworkers, others tried to find their respective cohorts, and the bewildered newcomers milled around looking for guidance.

Mafret moved among them, providing that guidance, tugging sleeves, pointing, directing.

By the time she was finished, everyone was thoroughly confused. It was obvious to O'Neill and Jackson that the groups were mixed beyond separation, looking at each other uncertainly.

The group O'Neill and Jackson found themselves in were obviously unfamiliar with each other. The looks received by the two men from Earth, dressed identically as they were to every other occupant of the servant house, were no less blank than the looks all the rest of them received. O'Neill's guess about the collars seemed to be correct; everyone else in their group wore them too.

The whole horde of them finally moved out, following in the sandaled footsteps of the oblivious Goa'uld strutting before them.

Unlike the time of their arrival, the Great Hall now was more like Grand Central Station, a scene of controlled chaos as hundreds of people streamed from one end of the room to the other, disappearing through large doorways. The Gate seemed to open to let newcomers in or to allow Goa'uld and Serpent Guards out on a fairly regular basis. O'Neill let go an involuntary sigh of relief. While the various work teams milled around, re-sorting themselves, and the tribute group wobbled like a disconnected compass, he and Jackson slipped away as if to join a bucket brigade, then ducked down a temporarily empty hallway.

It wasn't empty for more than a couple of seconds. Apparently their refuge led to a ready room for the Serpent Guards. Weapons lined the wall. Tables with chairs shoved carelessly into place occupied the center of the room.

And two Serpent Guards followed them, their helmets down, conversing quietly. They didn't seem particularly surprised at the sight of human slaves in their demesne.

O'Neill casually worked his way around behind them, checked to make sure no one else was coming down the hallway, and leaped, tigerlike.

The first Jaffa went sprawling, while the second's neck cracked with a brittle sound under O'Neill's hands. The man fell limp as a rag doll as O'Neill tossed him aside and executed a carefully calculated kick to the second man's throat just as he tried to push himself up and call an alarm. It was all over in less than ten seconds.

"Okay, Daniel," O'Neill said, as soon as he could catch his breath. He handed the other man one of the helmets. "We're not going to get any better chance than this. We've got to go find Nekhmet." The two of them stripped off their slave collars and replaced them, awkwardly, with Serpent Guard helmets and leather kilts, shoving the bodies into a weapons chest and placing the weapons it originally held on top. "We'll have a better chance if we split up. Then we can meet back here."

Daniel nodded, looking around rapidly, compulsively. Sha're was here. She had to be. She was—

Suddenly long, strong fingers were biting deep into his shoulders. "Dammit, Daniel. Look at me!"

Shocked, he had no choice. O'Neill's brown eyes were blazing into his.

"I know what you're thinking," the colonel said, his words quick and low. "Dammit, I thought the same thing. It's a chance to find Sha're, to find Skaara. It's a good bet they're here, somewhere.

"And *we're not gonna do that.*

"I've got two people depending on me—on us—to get them home from M'kwethet. Sam Carter and Teal'C are waiting for us. This is the only way back we've got, and we're gonna do it quick and quiet and keep our heads down."

Jackson swallowed hard and nodded, acknowledging both the thought and the order that countermanded it.

From that very hallway, they could hear the Gate belching open once again, the billowing of strange plasma settling back into itself.

"Synchronize your watch—no, wait, never mind." O'Neill looked disgusted with himself.

"If we're going to split up, don't we need to agree on a time when we'll meet?"

"Yeah, sure." O'Neill paused, and Jackson could see him thinking. "We don't have to worry about elapsed time through the wormhole. It doesn't seem to matter how far apart the worlds are, it always takes the same amount of time. Really funky physics." At Jackson's look of surprise, O'Neill shrugged sheepishly. "Yeah, well, I spent a lot of time looking at the pretty lights in the sky. Figured I might as well learn some astrophysics along the way. Don't tell Carter."

"It's Greek to me," Jackson assured him with a straight face, trying to shake the flash of resentment—and maybe even a bit of fear—he'd felt when O'Neill grabbed him.

"Oh, baaaaaaaaaad joke, Daniel." O'Neill stepped away, peered around the pillars. "Look. The main thing is to get all four of us back home, and that means retrieving Carter and Teal'C. That means we have to get our hands on a Key. Nekhmet isn't going to loan it to us just for the asking."

Daniel nodded, swallowing hard.

"We're going to have to kill him, and it's not going to be like killing those Jaffa, Daniel. It's going to be cold-blooded murder."

Jackson could feel his eyes widening.

He gave Daniel one last, searching look. *Don't go looking for Sha're.* He fretted momentarily, then let it go. "You do what you need to do, okay? Whichever of us gets through to bring them back—back to the guard-room, okay? We'll rendezvous there if we have to. Look, whichever of us gets through, we'll try to get back every three hours. The one still here has to have some idea when to be around. Every three hours, and we all go back home together. Right?"

Daniel swallowed. "Yes."

"Okay, then."

O'Neill went marching out into the hall as if he belonged there, with Daniel scrambling to catch up. The Gate guard nodded to the two of them, and O'Neill nodded back, raising a hand in salute without stopping, as they had seen the Guards do when they had first arrived. As they crossed the hall and the frescoes on the walls loomed larger, O'Neill muttered, "You go right, I'll go left. Good luck."

"How will I know whether you've already gone back to M'kwethet?" Daniel asked belatedly.

The helmet swung around toward him, expressionless and evil. "You'll know."

With that, O'Neill walked away, disappearing down the long hall to the left.

Taking a deep breath, Daniel veered to the right, in search of Nekhmet. Among other things.

He owed it to himself, to the Project, to gather as much data as possible while he was here, he told himself. He was an archaeologist. He had training in anthropology and folklore—that was one of the reasons he was a member of SG-1, after all. Who knew when such a golden opportunity would present itself again? Even if Saqqara wasn't the Goa'uld homeworld, it was obviously a major center for the aliens. He couldn't throw away the chance.

If he concentrated very, very hard on that thought, he could ignore the memory of O'Neill's blazing eyes as the colonel told him not to do exactly what he was going to do anyway. What he "had to do."

Find Sha're.

At least see her.

\* \* \*

O'Neill flowed forward, paying little attention to the wonders around him. He was looking for Nekhmet, and failing that, for any Jaffa who wore a Key. He didn't really think Daniel was going to be able to find one, or if he did, that the archaeologist would be able to get the apparatus; in fact, he was more or less certain that at this very moment Daniel was more likely thinking about his lost wife than anything else. It wasn't that Daniel didn't care deeply about the team, but he cared most about Sha're. O'Neill didn't really blame him. It was no accident that O'Neill had chosen to follow the corridor that Nekhmet had used the last time they'd seen him; he just hoped he wouldn't have to rescue the archaeologist too, once he got the others back.

And he *would* get the others back.

He spent just long enough in each room to determine that it was empty and then swept on, merciless as a hunting hawk.

Daniel was halfway across the Great Hall, going south, when he caught sight of the helmeted Serpent Guard heading for the guardroom. He had slipped his own stolen helmet off and left it tucked under the curtain, unable to tolerate the weight and the feel of the thing. Now he changed direction slightly to pass a little farther away from the Jaffa. He couldn't run; he could only hope that the Jaffa would simply not-see yet another human slave.

He'd managed to put a couple of columns between himself and the alcove by the time the Jaffa reached the control panel. He couldn't resist stopping to glance back. This was obviously the new panel operator. He spent a good two or three minutes looking around for the man he replaced, but apparently never looked behind the curtain. The Gate opened then, disrupting his search, and immediately thereafter another party of Jaffa showed up for transport. By that time the panel operator apparently decided that doing his job was more important than looking for his predecessor. Daniel sagged against the column, breathing a sigh of relief.

Opening his eyes again, he continued in the direction the arriving parties of Goa'uld had taken. He kept close to the walls, never meeting anyone's eyes, acutely aware of the puzzled glances occasionally cast his way. It was the damned glasses, it had to be. Jaffa, whose larval Goa'uld implants kept them superbly healthy, had no use for vision correction, and the technology didn't seem common to the human slaves.

The alternative was moving through a large blur, so he kept the glasses on. Full speed ahead and damn the torpedoes.

He passed a number of branching hallways and doorways before finally admitting that he had no idea where he was going. He needed a place to hide, first of all. Nekhmet had probably discovered that his case studies in the "aged and halt" category had gone missing, and instituted a search—a search that could well uncover the dead Jaffa. But he didn't have to hide for long, he decided. After all, when they'd come through the Gate with the tribute, he hadn't seen anyone at the control panel, so as O'Neill had pointed out, obviously it wasn't staffed all the time. He'd wait until the operator was gone, then open the Gate again, and hope that O'Neill and the others were ready.

Having resigned himself, he turned the corner of the next high arched doorway he came to, seeking shelter.

What he saw next stopped him dead in his tracks. The only thing he could think of was the words all students of Egyptology read at the very beginning of their studies, read with yearning and awe and profound envy of the man who had made, in 1922, the definitive discovery in their field:

*As he peered through the small hole, Carter was at first unable to distinguish specific objects, because the pale light cast off by the candle flickered constantly. But he soon realised that he was looking, not at wall paintings, but at three-dimensional objects: they appeared to be enormous gold bars stacked against the wall opposite the entrance. Dumbfounded, transfixed, he just stood there muttering: "wonderful, marvellous, my God, wonderful!"*

But instead of looking at the jumbled relics of a dead boy-king, he found himself, like a mouse at a banquet, looking up at the very image of the Son of the Living Sun, Beloved of Aten, the Mighty Bull Enthroned in Splendor, Living Forever: Apophis. In a portrait at least forty feet tall.

*So* that's *what they use all those feathers for,* the voice in the back of his mind observed.

# CHAPTER FIFTEEN

*If it weren't for the immediate issue of the survival of the team,* O'Neill thought, *this would be a terrific opportunity to spy.* He'd have to put that in his report to Hammond when it was all over. If they could get their hands on a portable DHD—*when,* he corrected himself—they'd never have to worry again about getting trapped this way, or finding themselves on worlds where the DHD might be damaged beyond repair. It would be a terrific addition to Earth's arsenal.

And who knew what else was here? The mind control devices of the Goa'uld, like the ribbon devices they wore around their hands that produced devastating energies, were most likely forever beyond their reach. But the Jaffa had started out human, and they couldn't use them either, so there had to be a lot of stuff, energy weapons like Teal'C's staff and so on, that Earth *could* use. And adapt. And improve. Human beings had always been really good at finding newer and better ways to kill.

The trouble was, most of the time he had no idea what he was looking at and couldn't take time to window-shop. One room was full of heavy, metal, pointy things that had to be weapons of some sort, but he had no idea how they worked. Once he found himself looking out a back door into a garden as exquisite and extensive under a glorious blue sky as anything produced at Versailles, but he couldn't see anyone out admiring it and there wasn't any cover among the graded walkways and cheerful fountains anyway. He ducked back in and kept going.

Even Goa'uld had to have a support infrastructure. Kitchens, to produce food for masters and slaves. Laundries—at least he supposed they were laundries, judging from the clothing hanging in rack upon rack, though there wasn't any humidity or smell of steam. Or perhaps there was and he just couldn't smell it through the heavy Serpent Guard helmet. Once he was fairly sure no one was around, he retracted the serpent head, breathing a sigh of claustrophobic relief as it slid back and collapsed into a collar around his neck. Anyone seeing him now would know instantly he wasn't the real thing—no mark upon his forehead—but at least he could look around without turning his head.

But this wasn't going to get him anywhere. This random wandering was taking hours; he was getting hungry and thirsty and frustrated. Nekhmet could be anywhere, but O'Neill was willing to bet he wouldn't be hanging around the laundry room. He was going to have to take the direct approach, which appealed to him anyway.

Heading away from the laundries, he moved back in the direction of the kitchens. If he hadn't seen Mafret's, he wouldn't have recognized these as food preparation areas either; they consisted of a series of rooms with large white cabinets along the walls and large granite-looking tables scattered about. By this time several slaves were beginning to busy themselves, pulling covered dishes out of the cabinets and placing them on trays.

O'Neill hesitated, then took a deep breath, removed the Serpent Guard helmet, and dropped the energy staff behind it. After a moment's thought he also got rid of the gray metal collar around his neck.

Adopting his very best imitation of servile fear, he approached one of the men who seemed to be directing matters.

"My lord," he whined, "I beg you to help me. I am ordered to take food to my lord Nekhmet, and I don't know where he is."

The servant, an older, gray-haired man, stifled a laugh as he looked up at O'Neill. "You don't know where he *is*? Are you joking?"

O'Neill stared down at his feet. "No, lord. I'm new, just come from M'kwethet. Please, lord, I'm afraid they'll punish me." He tried to imagine himself as Oliver Twist. *Please, sir, may I have some more?* It didn't help. However, *Look, buddy, I asked you a question* probably would help even less.

"If you don't want to be punished, you'll wipe that look off your face. The lords don't want to see their servants sucking lemons." The kitchen master looked around the room, which was beginning to fill with activity as more and more people poured in, preparing food, embellishing food, bearing it away to some unknown destination. "I suppose this means my lord isn't eating with the others of the high Jaffa. He didn't happen to say what he wanted, did he?"

O'Neill swallowed hard and shook his head. "Bread?" he tried to suggest helpfully.

"You idiot." But the overseer said it in an absentminded, almost kindly fashion, far more interested in watching the minor commotion at the other end of the room caused by humans carrying, of all things, a helmet and an energy staff. "Where did they get those things? Here, you! Get rid of that *now*. Are you *trying* to get killed? As for you—" he wheeled back to O'Neill, "take those cakes there. My lord's chamber is at the end of the Hall of Serpents, in the northwest wing. Go at once. You'll find he doesn't like to be kept waiting."

*Let them eat cake,* O'Neill thought, as he took the plate and started down the hall again. He'd missed breakfast, and the cakes were good, with some kind of cherry filling

that wasn't too sweet. He remembered an archway out of
the Gate room that was framed in a mosaic of writhing
snakes. That must be the Hall of Serpents. Rearranging
the remaining comestibles, he moved as fast as possible
without attracting attention, pausing only to glance at the
traffic in the central Hall. There was no sign of Daniel.

Nekhmet's chamber had the distinction of being a pri-
vate suite, with an entry chamber, a sleeping room, and a
curtained-off bathing room off to one side. It was empty
when he arrived. He set the tray on an enameled table and
looked through every room, checking the tops of the deli-
cately carved furniture for discarded jewelry or, failing
that, some kind of weapon.

No such luck, naturally.

He was about to toss the drawers in the sleeping room
when he heard voices in the hallway and faded back into
the bathing area. Nekhmet entered with two companions,
who exclaimed with pleasure at the sight of the cakes. The
three of them settled immediately to stuff themselves,
meanwhile exchanging gossip about no one O'Neill had
ever heard of. Pressing himself back against the wall as
hard as possible, he twitched the curtain open with his
little finger and risked a glance into the room. Yes;
Nekhmet was still wearing the leather brace. He blew out a
long, silent breath and kept very, very still.

*Marvelous things.*

Gold everywhere: gold leaf on the pillars, in the pat-
terned ceilings, on the furniture. Gold, most especially,
lining the portrait. Gold catching the light and throwing it
back and hurting the eyes, so much that Daniel slipped his
glasses off in self-defense and tucked them into his shirt.
He moved around the side of the room, keeping to the
walls like Chundra the rat, pausing every few steps to look
at something new or to dodge a slave or a Jaffa. They
ignored him. He barely noticed.

The furniture was carved, the arms and legs representing lions' paws, the backs supporting bas-relief landscapes and portraits. He saw a lamp—or at least a round, glowing globe—with a wax cone atop it. As the wax melted, heavy perfumes were released into the air.

Statues, three times life-size, representing pharaohs—or Goa'uld—striding forward, hands lifted, ribbon weapons embracing their arms, lined the walls. They reminded him of the Assyrian sculptures in the British Museum as much as of the heroic statuary of the Egyptian kings. The statues were painted and gilded, with skin tones ranging from flat black to pearl white, and every shade in between. The faces, he noticed with some peering, were identical under the identical headcloth-and-uraeus, as if the individual features were irrelevant. The kilts were real cloth, pleated to a knife edge, starched into immobility. The oversized sandals were real leather, embedded with gems and more gold.

At the head of the room was a large platform. On it were three empty thrones, the arms in the form of lions, the legs in the shape of lions' paws, all gilded; the Eye of Horus marked the back of each of them. The largest was slightly behind the other two.

Behind the empty thrones were the fan slaves, waving massive fans of ostrich plumes to keep the thickly scented air moving. It made the feather portrait of Apophis tremble, as if it were alive. Even without his glasses he could see the sweat glistening on their faces. They wore feather headdresses, too. The Goa'uld had the technology to air-condition the entire place, he was certain. But air-conditioning just didn't have that groveling odor associated with it.

Off to one side of the thrones, shockingly out of place, was evidence that the aliens could dispense with mere humankind if they wanted to. A large globe, hovering in midair, stood waiting for power; a Goa'uld communication device. It was blank at the moment. Daniel shook his head as if in denial and moved on, slowly circling the room, sometimes sneaking his glasses back on for a quick focus and then putting them away again in an attempt to alleviate the ferocious glow.

The paintings on the walls were of hunting scenes, the same scenes he would have expected to find in a well-preserved tomb in the Valley of the Kings, except that these pictures were vibrant and fresh. And interspersed with the images of Egyptian kings riding chariots in pursuit of lions and antelope were scenes of those same kings pursuing creatures that had never evolved on Earth, creatures with odd joints and sideways jaws and manes like cilia. The pictures of hunters on the river using cats to retrieve showed the animals bringing not only ducks but strange fragile orange butterfly-looking things to their masters. The figures were not merely the animal-headed Egyptian gods, but alien in their entirety; and the figures following after the kings wore the helmets of the Serpent Guards, the cartouches of the Jaffa, and the crossed slits in their bellies were clearly defined.

He could spend the rest of his life here, he thought deliriously, studying, recording, analyzing. He could reconstruct the contact with the Earth of ancient Egypt, stretching from the predynastic era to at least the Eighteenth Dynasty, see the effects of Egyptian culture on that of the Goa'uld—

A little smile played over his lips. So much for the impact of ancient starfarers on his homeworld; from the looks of it, cultural diffusion had osmosed in very much the opposite direction. The art, clothing—even the music, the sounds of flute and sistrum and soft drumming—could have come straight from the souks of Alexandria, barely changed over the millennia.

Shouts coming from the arched entryway finally pulled his attention away from the wall paintings. A team of

Jaffa marched in, carrying a body on a bier. The courtiers gasped; the servants pressed back against the walls, trying to be invisible; even the fan bearers froze in place.

They'd found the dead Serpent Guards.

*You do what you need to do, okay? Whichever of us gets through to bring them back—back to the guardroom, okay? We'll rendezvous there if we have to.*

Daniel Jackson adopted the bearing of the midservants, the ones between the lowliest slaves and the aristocracy of service. He found an empty tray on a table, picked it up and kept his head down. A cup set into a wall niche provided another prop. The excitement caused by the discovery of the body had rippled out from the Throne Room, driving him deeper and deeper into the Goa'uld palace.

On the one hand, it was still a wonderful opportunity for a scientist to explore. On the other, he had to find Nekhmet, or someone else with a bracelet, to operate the Gate.

On the third hand, the Gate was probably *very* heavily guarded right now.

On the fourth hand, that gave him a great excuse to probe deeper, to see if he could find any sign of Sha're.

The only trouble was that he only had two hands, and this was exactly the kind of thing O'Neill had warned him against. He had to focus on the team getting back home again.

A squad of Jaffa, their expanded helmets making them look like two-legged cobras, marched by double-time, their energy staffs held out before them, ready for use. Daniel pressed himself into the wall to let them go by, his fingers white against the gold of the tray; the cup upon it rattled.

He had tried several times to circle back, but each time the Jaffa were there before him, blocking the way. None of the human slaves were allowed access to the Gate room. Several times he thought the Serpent Guards followed him suspiciously as he tried again and again to get past them. Once he found himself hiding in the Great House's feather room, desperately trying to keep from sneezing as the Guards pushed around huge baskets of feathers with their energy staffs. It really *was* too much like the Marx brothers. And all of it for nothing; he couldn't find Nekhmet, much less Sha're or Apophis or even a larval nursery.

Eventually even the strain of hiding, a mouse in a clowder of serpent-headed cats, couldn't overcome the need for rest. He found himself back in the feather-storage room, staggering from sheer stress-induced exhaustion. *Nobody seems to come here,* he thought foggily. Surely he could sit down for just a moment, behind this gigantic woven basket, and lean his head against . . .

He woke with a jolt, some undetermined time later, a yellow pinfeather tickling his nose. From deep within the building came an eerily familiar wailing. Blinking, he stood up and caught the woven basket before it fell. No, this was—this wasn't Egypt, nor was it Abydos, but that wailing was exactly the same. He shuddered with a sudden chill at the thought of the sounds of desolation, of mourning echoing not just across deserts of sand but of stars as well. Someone had died.

He wondered momentarily what had happened to the tribute, then forced himself to stop worrying about it. Those kids—and kids they were, after all—weren't his responsibility; they'd had the chance to change their minds and had elected to be part of their world's sacrifice anyway. His worry was his own team.

*And, of course, Sha're,* the voice in the back of his mind pointed out, however far beyond his reach she might be.

The feeling of circling aimlessly, unable to return to the Gate, unable to locate either Nekhmet or the nursery where Sha're would be, overwhelmed him for a moment. Maybe this wasn't the Goa'uld homeworld after all. Maybe it really *was* all for nothing.

Who had died? Apophis? He shook his head. Nothing would be that easy. Someone important, though. That kind of mourning was reserved for chiefs, leaders.

Voices?

Had O'Neill succeeded?

It would fit the circumstances.

If so, he'd better get back to the guardroom. He couldn't just stand here; he'd better start being decisive.

Although even being decisive wasn't going to do either him or O'Neill a heck of a lot of good if the Stargate was being guarded by Serpent Guards.

What would O'Neill do?

Make some smart-aleck remark, no doubt. And then create some diversion that would save the day.

Another squad of snake-helmed Jaffa came by, and he executed a swift right-face and entered yet another supply room filled with row upon row of pure white wax candles and several large jars that sloshed when he jostled them.

Candles. And oil. Now *there* was an idea. If only he could be sure its time had come. . . . The Gate room wasn't that far from the storage areas. He made his preparations and headed back to see if he could tell what was going on.

The Hall of the Gate was frothing with activity, so much that it spilled out into the halls leading away. Daniel had to push his way past excited servants.

The Gate abruptly began to move, and the panicked operator at the console was yelling at a senior Guard that it wasn't his fault, someone must be operating a remote, the system was already engaged and he couldn't break in. Daniel couldn't spot Jack anywhere, but a squad of Serpent Guards was being hastily assembled to stand watch over the Gate—presumably if someone was operating it, that meant it was supposed to be used. The inner ring slid smoothly back and forth. Daniel pushed closer, hoping to be able to find Jack, to make a break for it when the colonel did, and then paused.

If the Jaffa had the sense to watch the Gate's destination being dialed in, they could identify it. They would follow Jack and probably destroy M'kwcthct. A distraction was required *right now,* and he didn't have time to get back to his little booby trap.

He whipped off his glasses and screamed at the top of his lungs, "Fire! Fire in the Throne Room! The Great One's portrait is burning!"

The servants surrounding him jerked around to stare in shock. He pointed and ran back toward the hall that led to the room with the feather portrait. Someone else—a woman—picked up the cry.

In moments dozens of people were repeating the alarm, surging back to the perimeters of the room and then out again to the hall. Even the senior Serpent Guard's helmet looked momentarily indecisive, and as he gave contradictory commands the Gate spun, back and forth and back again. Someone else shrieked that they had lost track of the chevrons.

One of the squad lined up on either side of the Gate shouted that he would find out where the Gate led. He sounded very heroic and self-sacrificing. The other Guards clearly thought he was nuts; Daniel could hear one say something about "the Emptiness."

Daniel was getting dangerously near the edge of a knot of people, too close to open space. He looked about for some place to blend in.

A hand touched his shoulder, and he spun around, his belly suddenly a lump of ice.

"You are mad," Mafret said. "But it is a strong, strange madness. Come."

"They're gonna find out the feathers aren't burning any

second now," Daniel whispered. "We've gotta give him time—"

"Ah, but the feathers do burn," she said, barely moving her lips. "A wonderful idea. Come quickly."

Behind them, the Gate billowed open, and the volunteer threw himself through just as the console operator regained control and shut it tightly behind him.

This time, as Jack O'Neill tumbled through the M'kwethet Gate, the first thing he did was to take off the helmet he had retrieved. The second was to look for the DHD. It still wasn't there.

This time, though, he had a DHD of his very own. The damn thing weighed as much as a medium barbell, but it worked. He'd managed to manually rotate the inner dial, exactly like a combination lock, and once he'd pushed the right button on top, the thing had actually worked. Based on the way the Jaffa had formed up to guard the Gate, though, he wasn't going to have that kind of luck on the way back. Daniel wouldn't cut and run for Earth until he knew the others were all right. If only the kid had been where he was supposed to be when he was supposed to be there—but whatever that distraction had been had worked beautifully.

And the mini-DHD not only worked, but it brought him to the right place. That remark about the Emptiness was a little scary, in hindsight, but before him stood a very small contingent of M'kwethet citizens finishing up their daily shopping, alerted to his entrance by the characteristic plasma roar of a wormhole being established. This time they recognized him immediately.

It was twilight on M'kwethet, and most of the shops in the little square were closed and shuttered for the night. He could still see the remains of the bunting and banners that marked the recent ceremonies, smell the spicy scents of the evening meal being prepared.

The M'kwethet made no effort to take him captive, to alert guards. They simply stared at him, passive, resentful. No one even asked him about the sons and daughters he had accompanied to Saqqara.

He was, he decided, thoroughly fed up with M'kwethet. He wanted to find Carter and Teal'C and get the hell off this world that was so committed to appeasing the monsters that fed on it.

Unfortunately, Carter and Teal'C were not conveniently in sight, waiting to be shuttled back to the necessary intermediate stop on the way home. And no one was stepping up to volunteer their location.

Well, if anyone would know, he'd bet on the Council, the Rejected Ones. And if they didn't tell him, he would show them what being rejected was really all about. Jumping down lightly from the platform, he headed across the square to the banquet hall.

# CHAPTER SIXTEEN

Of all the inhabitants of M'kwethet, only Alizane Skill-keeper had a hope in hell of impressing Jack O'Neill. At least she wasn't afraid to lose her temper.

And she was doing so, spectacularly.

"You are," she announced, "a lying, thieving, murdering monster. Your people stole our children. They stole our hope of peace."

She was facing him across the table, leaning forward on her hands, bristling with fury. He advanced to the other side, forcing her to stand up straight in order to look at him. It didn't do anything to help the situation.

It was the same room they'd used earlier. Looking around it, at the little group of huddled teenagers standing protectively around Carter and Teal'C, at the tiny contingent of strong-arms backing up the red-clad Council, he couldn't help but compare it to Saqqara. Even the servant house of Ahmose was bigger than this, and in better repair. The servant house, for example, wouldn't dare have a stain on the ceiling betraying a leak in the roof, or chips out of the marble columns.

He hadn't particularly noticed those things before, or if he had, they'd lent the place a certain charming antiquity. Now, having seen the Goa'uld world, he realized this place looked shabby and poor.

He wondered if Alizane felt that way about her home-world, having spent almost two years on Saqqara.

He doubted that was uppermost in her mind at the moment. As soon as he entered the Agora, Jareth had spotted him, escorted him into a back room. Shortly thereafter Alizane and Karlanan had arrived, followed by five teenagers and his missing teammates. None of them looked bruised, at least, but Carter's face was wooden and she kept blinking hard. Teal'C didn't have his staff—he must have given it up voluntarily. He looked subtly unhappy, too.

Alizane was still talking. "And now you say the Great Ones are unhappy with their tribute. Whose head do you think their wrath will fall upon?"

He waited out her rage. She was the spokesman for the Council; both Jareth and Karlanan hung back, the older man wringing his hands with distress while the younger one sulked like the bully he was.

"You claim to have the good of our children at heart, but look at them. There were six who fled their sworn duty, their honor to be candidates for tribute. Now there are only five. Where is Maesen?"

"I don't—" he began.

Carter cleared her throat. "Um, ma'am—"

They turned in unison to look at her, Alizane glaring, O'Neill inquiring.

Carter faced O'Neill, standing at attention. He saw the sick look in her eyes and knew what had happened before she even began to speak.

"Sir, I regret to inform you that one of the individuals under my care and protection became ill. We think she—she caught cold. Despite all our efforts Maesen apparently developed pneumonia, and she died. Because of the unusual nature of the illness I felt it prudent to bury her on site rather than transport her body back to the city."

Got sick.

Died.

Of all the stupid things to happen on this mission, to have a kid catch cold and die was the stupidest.

He gave Carter an acknowledging nod, hoping she caught the understanding he tried to convey at the same time. She stepped back into the little crowd; the tension in her face had eased, not entirely, but at least a little.

"Sick?" Alizane's jaw dropped. "How could she be sick? We don't have sickness here anymore."

"And apparently you don't have resistance to viruses either, ma'am." Carter managed to keep her voice even. "Markhtin got sick too, but he seems to have recovered."

Jareth, Alizane, and Karlanan shared a bewildered glance. "Vi russes? What are those?"

O'Neill heaved a sigh. "Things that make you sick," he said. He wasn't about to try to introduce contagion theory to this world.

"One of you gave Maesen this vi. Russ?"

Carter winced. "It might have been a function of Daniel's cold; she'd have to have been terribly vulnerable, with no immune system at all—"

"So you killed her. You murdered her—"

One of the runaway teenagers, a young woman with long braided blond hair and a silver-gray walking stick, stepped out of the crowd to advance on Alizane.

"How dare you?" she snapped. "How dare you accuse her of the death of my friend, when you—yes, you, my own aunt—would send us all to our deaths. We've seen the Goa'uld larvae. That one"—she indicated Teal'C—"he carries one, and we all saw. Is that the kind of child you'd have Maesen carry beneath her heart? She's better off dead."

Alizane turned white. "Clein'dori, you don't know what you're saying. You don't understand. We don't carry larvae—"

"Yes, I do. I was there, and you weren't. Isn't that what you always told us when we were little, about what it was like serving the Goa'uld? We would never really understand until we were there ourselves. Well, I was there with Maesen, and she died alone and afraid, but she died *herself*."

Jareth tried to interpose himself between the two angry women—never a good tactic, O'Neill felt like telling him. "If Maesen had died on Saqqara, it would have been a death full of honor, a death in the service of her people, keeping them safe. We all went prepared to die. It is a fair price to pay."

He gestured at O'Neill. "Ask him. Ask your new friends if they're willing to die for their countrymen. And then let him explain to us the difference, if there is any, and why they encourage you to hide from your duty!"

A little silence fell as they all turned to stare at O'Neill.

"Well?" Clein'dori asked at last. Her fingers tightened around the long, heavy stick. She looked like she knew how to use it and wouldn't be at all afraid to. "Does your world ask you to die in its service?"

He closed his eyes, then snapped them open again to banish the images of those kids with missing limbs, shredded bowels hanging out, screaming and crying for their mothers. Of his own people gagging and retching and suffocating in gas attacks in Iraq.

"No," he said slowly, "my country doesn't ask me to die in its service." Out of the corner of his eye he caught a sudden movement by Carter, reacting to his words, and the equally sudden stillness by Teal'C.

"My country asks me to *fight* in its service, to keep it free. It doesn't want me to die, even though we all know that might happen. Dying for my country isn't my job.

"My job is to make sure the other poor dumb bastard dies for *his* country."

It might not be very palatable, but it was true. It was true for the Jaffa Guards whose necks he'd broken hours ago, and for the tank troops in his sights as he flew over Iraq, and for the Viet Cong years ago.

"We fight to protect our people, to keep them free from threats like the Goa'uld."

It wasn't his job to second-guess the morality of war, but to wage it. When he was lucky, the morality was easy and clear-cut. He supposed he was lucky in that respect in this war against the Goa'uld, but that didn't make those poor Jaffa at the Saqqara Gate any more alive.

The red-clad Councilors were staring at him uncomprehendingly. He shook his head. "Look, I told you when I left here that I'd be back for my people. That's all I want. Just let us go to the Gate and as soon as it opens, we'll be outta here." The first time check had already passed. He wondered if Daniel was still alive.

"But where . . ." Jareth began haltingly. "Where is our justice? If you go, we are left with only our dead, our broken promise to the Goa'uld. Should we simply let you go?"

*Yep, since you asked my opinion, that's exactly what you should do.* At least, O'Neill thought wryly, he had the sense not to say that out loud. He wasn't sure what to say anymore.

Teal'C stirred, rather like a mountain considering the possibility of an earthquake, and came forward. The kids gave him a wide berth, even Clein'dori. "There is justice," he rumbled. "You have lost a child. We have failed in our mission. We must return home and tell our leaders that we were not able to follow their orders."

Alizane's eyes lit up as if the prospect delighted her. "They will punish you, then. They will punish you severely."

"As do all leaders when their followers fail," Teal'C agreed. He turned to O'Neill, bowing his head in the nearest thing to a humble gesture O'Neill had ever seen the big man make. "I have failed you, my leader. We both have failed you."

O'Neill caught on instantly. "And you'll be punished for

it, of course. If our leaders let me live long enough to see to it." Behind Teal'C, out of the line of sight of the Councilors, he could see enlightenment dawn on Carter, who grabbed Clein'dori and whispered urgently in her ear. Clein'dori, who was about to protest once more, subsided, looking at first puzzled and then nearly as wickedly delighted as Alizane. O'Neill wished they could keep track of the blond kid—she obviously had potential. Maybe she would grow up to lead a coup d'état against the Councilors and the whole tribute system.

And maybe the Goa'uld would wipe them all out.

Not his responsibility. His responsibility was Carter and Teal'C and Jackson. Period.

"That seems fair," Karlanan offered. "If your leaders kill you."

"I'm certain that will cross their minds," O'Neill said. With Hammond, that was a sure bet. The General had a low tolerance for screwups, and this one was a prize example.

"Go, then," Alizane decided, without bothering to consult her fellow Councilors. "Wait, and when the Gate opens, go through it. And never come back again."

"That I can promise you," O'Neill said feelingly. "For your part—" he hesitated and looked at her long and hard. "What were you going to do to your children? One of them has died already for defying your ways." He felt like gagging as he said it, but Alizane's commitment to punishment as example left him nearly certain what the Council had planned for the remaining five. "Surely they have been punished enough. They can never be Chosen again, can they?"

*Let them live,* he was suggesting. *Let them live without honor as you measure honor, but let them live.*

The five young people standing around Carter understood exactly what he was saying. Not all of them accepted it in the same fashion. One of the twins looked indignant at the very idea. The blond girl was remote and thoughtful, watching her elders decide her fate. He had a feeling that she would have a few things of her own to say about it.

*Live to fight another day,* he tried to tell them, without allowing the Council to see that in his eyes.

Alizane turned to Jareth. "What do you think?"

Karlanan growled, "They must be punished."

"Won't the memory of the loss of their friend be punishment enough?"

They didn't really want to kill the kids. It was part of the generally submissive nature of the culture. Blood-thirstiness just wasn't in them.

It didn't take long for them to acquiesce.

O'Neill gathered up his team.

# CHAPTER SEVENTEEN

Carter paced around the M'kwethet Gate, pausing occasionally to peer through the open circle as if she could see another world on the other side.

"Siddown, Captain," O'Neill said wearily, checking the action on his sidearm. It was spotless. So was his rifle. They should have been, considering he'd broken them down for cleaning at least three times so far. "We're not going to go just yet. I want to give it time to cool down there. And you can't open the Gate by using up all your energy that way."

"It is possible that Daniel Jackson was discovered and killed on Saqqara," Teal'C observed.

"No, it's not." O'Neill dismissed the possibility with finality. "He's fine. He's waiting for us."

"Sir, if we're going to wait, I'd really like to talk to the kids again." Carter was sitting, fidgeting. Then she bounced to her feet as if she'd heard something. "I feel like I failed them."

"Unlikely, considering you took the best course of action available to you at the time," Teal'C pointed out.

Carter glared and resumed pacing. The colonel got to his feet, looking over the expanse of the city one more time.

"I don't think I've ever been so glad to leave a place," he murmured.

"They're gonna do something awful to those kids," Carter whispered.

"Sit *down,* Captain!" O'Neill had had enough of her nervous energy. She was doing too good a job of reflecting his own inner turmoil. The second time check had passed while he was still arguing with Alizane. He hated the idea of waiting for more time to pass, but he couldn't change the rules now. Meanwhile he and Teal'C examined every part of the leather arm guard.

Around them, the life of M'kwethet flowed serenely on. The shops were closed. The moons rose.

A lithe figure ran across the silvered square and stood at the bottom of the three steps.

"Why aren't you gone?" Clein'dori asked. "I thought you were going to leave."

*We were talking about justice,* O'Neill thought. He turned the leather brace over and over in his hands.

"I am so sorry," Carter said, helplessness apparent in her voice. "I am *so* sorry about Maesen."

"I know you tried," the young woman said. "But now you have a way to leave and you're leaving us behind until they come again. We have no way to escape."

"Your elders would not use it," Teal'C rumbled. "They would return this device to the Goa'uld in hope of earning their favor."'

"I wouldn't," she answered. The light caught her long braid and for a moment her hair was white instead of blond, like a band of silver around her brow.

They could really use the technology on Earth.

Earth already had a DHD.

"Let me show you how this works," a voice said, and O'Neill found himself striding down the steps. "I'll give you the symbols to open the Gate to—to the Nox world. They'll keep you safe."

"I want to go to your world."

He couldn't take the time to explain about the iris. "It won't work to Earth," he said. "We have to use it to go back to Saqqara. But here, watch how this goes—"

It was late, really late. Mafret had found a place for him beyond the Hall and told him not to move.

There were fewer search parties now, though. Jackson forced himself to move past the Jaffa as if he had every right, or at least every obligation, to head directly for the little guardroom off the main hall. The Jaffa and the human servants never spared him a glance.

The three-hour check-in had passed again. It had given him time to set up his desperate attempt at a second diversion. He didn't know if it would even work or, if it did, whether this would be the time they picked to come through. But if it did, and they did, he'd have to be right there to take advantage of what he sincerely hoped would be at least minor hysteria.

The Gate room was full again. Three Jaffa stood guard around the DHD. Eight more, on either side of the Gate, were at rigid attention.

He debated hiding in a handy alcove, remembered where the last one had led to, and decided against it. The senior Serpent Guard performed a last inspection of the squad at the Gate.

Ten deep breaths later, he was beginning to worry about whether it was going to work after all. He bit his lip, thinking about going back to see if—

The Gate opened.

A double line of Jaffa came through the shimmering pool. The waiting occupants of the room all turned expectantly to the open wormhole.

*Oh, God*, Daniel prayed. *Not now. Not yet.*

A long parade started through the Gate. The Jaffa were followed by musicians and dancing girls, by more Goa'uld.

A roar of greeting went up as the end of the procession came through. Every living thing in the Gate room not actively involved in the procession fell to its knees.

Rooted to the mosaic floor, Daniel watched as Apophis came through the M'kwethet Gate, with his Queen, Sha're, beside him.

Her eyes were outlined with kohl and shadow, her hair dressed in a fall of rich brown curls. On her head she wore a tiara of gold, studded with turquoise and carnelian, with slender strings of gold fanning over her face as a veil. A matching collar stretched from her clavicles to her nipples, a fan of slender golden strips jointed together. Around her waist was a wide belt of matching strips that chimed as she walked, as her hips moved. From her belt fell a sheer skirt of glowing white.

His lips parted, forming her name. He wanted to run to her, shake recognition back into her eyes.

He did nothing.

The procession made its way across the great hall and south, toward the hastily repaired Throne Room. The waiting audience followed, for the most part; the Serpent Guards flanking the Gate proceeded after, along with one of those assigned to the DHD.

He watched her go, and he did nothing, thinking blankly, *She wasn't even here. All the time I spent looking for her, and she wasn't even here.*

By the time all of them had passed through the arched doorway to the Throne Room, the Gate had settled down to stillness once again.

The royal procession was barely out of sight when an explosion shook the building and a wall of greasy black smoke billowed from the next hall over.

At the same time, the Gate billowed open again.

Screams echoed from the depths of the building. The rest of the people in the Great Hall called out frantically. A Serpent Guard raced out of the ready room, looked around and yelled to the two still on the DHD. The three started toward the wall of greasy orange flame gouting up from the arched hallway opening.

Daniel faded back into the ready room and snatched up the nearest energy staffs. Charging one, he ran back out and into the DHD alcove.

The room was filling with smoke. He coughed, his eyes watering.

One of the Serpent Guards turned back at the unscheduled sound of the Gate opening. Daniel raised the staff and shot him. More shadows moved uncertainly in the smoke.

"Come on come on come on," he chanted, as if it were a spell that would bring them through. "Come *on*, dammit . . ."

Tumbling through the Gate, without a scrap of the dignity of the Goa'uld, came the other three members of SG-1. They managed to be back on their feet by the time they got to the bottom of the platform steps.

Daniel heaved energy staffs at them as if the weapons were javelins. The team could barely see them—indeed, one staff hit Teal'C in the ankle before he could blink away the fumes to see it. It would take a few minutes for the Gate to shut down, a few deadly minutes before he could encode the symbols for Earth.

"Daniel!" O'Neill yelled. "You there?"

He started to yell back, doubled over with a fit of coughing.

"Never mind!"

The wormhole from M'kwethet shut down, leaving a sudden pool of silence broken only by harsh panting from the combatants and moans from the injured. None of his team, Daniel was glad to see. He started to stand to input the symbols for Earth. He had to get them through before the iris was shut again.

Out of the smoke came more Serpent Guards, members

of the royal escort, helmets up, eyes glowing. O'Neill, Carter, and Teal'C laid down covering fire, waiting for him to open the Gate and join them. The Guards were firing blindly, away from the DHD. Behind them, still more shadows moved. Daniel couldn't tell whether they were stray slaves, courtiers, Jaffa, Guards, or Goa'uld; it didn't matter.

The Serpent Guards greeted him with a concerted volley. One bolt of energy caught his upper arm. He could smell the melted metal of his slave collar as it liquefied and curled into the muscle; he could hear a scream of agony coming from somewhere; he just couldn't feel anything.

He couldn't feel the symbols under his hands. The panels wouldn't depress. He tried leaning on them, but his arm wouldn't support him. A thin trickle of red rolled down his arm, following the muscles and the bones, down his wrist, pooling in one of the symbols. He must have been—

"Daniel!" The word was frantic, angry. He looked up to see O'Neill trying to edge over to him.

*No,* he thought. *That won't work. I need to input the signals. Then go over there. To the Gate.*

Their opponents were advancing. Carter and Teal'C were firing steadily, remorselessly into the line of Serpent Guards.

He managed to slap the symbol again, weakly, and this time felt it give under his hand. The Gate spun. The first chevron locked into place.

Another. He was beginning to feel—something—in his arm. All things considered, he'd rather not, he thought, but the shock was beginning to wear off. The Serpent Guards had shifted their attention, were concentrating their fire now on the narrow alcove entrance.

Another.

Another.

The panels were getting slippery, sticky with blood.

He could hear shouting coming from behind the Guards, as if panicky orders and protests were crossing each other.

Another.

O'Neill had managed, somehow, to get past the line of fire, probably using the dead bodies of Guards, as well as the smoke, for cover. The smoke was beginning to clear, Daniel saw; at least, his vision was less hazy now. More blurry, perhaps.

Another.

O'Neill was there, firing steadily at his side, waiting for him to hit the last symbol. He took a deep breath to try to clear his head and staggered.

"Okay, Daniel," the colonel said. "Let's get this done and clear out of here. C'mon, buddy. Almost home."

Almost.

Smoke still danced, shifting as if being pulled back and forth by ostrich feather fans, and his eyes were watering, so he wasn't sure what he saw, standing behind the line of Guards. It might have been his imagination.

It might have been a woman dressed in white, wearing a golden tiara, her eyes for one instant warm once more, her hand lifted as if reaching for him.

His useless hand lay on the last symbol, and he blinked and looked up again as a last veil of smoke swirled. Yes. She was definitely there.

He propped himself in place and pushed.

The Gate spun.

O'Neill yelled, grabbed his good arm, and began dragging him to the edge of the alcove.

The signal. He had to send the signal, otherwise they'd be smashed against the iris on the other side of the wormhole. Falling to his knees, he triggered the device. O'Neill grabbed his arm and began half-lifting him to the Gate, firing randomly with the energy staff as he did so.

Teal'C and Carter redoubled their fire, never glancing

back at the plasma wash of unspace billowing through the gate as the wormhole to Earth opened.

He tried to help. Tried to walk, at least, if not run, to the welcoming silvery shimmer. The blue mosaic beneath his feet ran together like water. He stared coughing, a deep, hard rattle from his guts.

The other two rose into a crouch and began scuttling, backing them to the Gate.

He nearly slipped to the floor as O'Neill shifted, trying to fire the energy staff and discard it at the same time, and took a last look back toward the hall of the Throne Room.

She was there. Watching.

He lost consciousness then anyway, so it didn't matter if he called to her.

*There does not appear to be any military or economic advantage to pursuing any further relationship with the people of the world called M'kwethet. Their government is vested in sustaining a subservient relationship with the Goa'uld. They demonstrated no interest in exploring areas of mutual assistance or defense.*

O'Neill sighed and pinched the bridge of his nose. They didn't even have coordinates for Saqqara. They'd gotten exactly nothing out of this mission, nothing at all. Not even the portable DHD. He was going to have a hell of a time explaining that one to Hammond in the morning.

They couldn't win them all, he tried to tell himself. They were lucky not to have lost everything.

Some, perhaps, had lost everything all over again.

Carter had learned one more time the hard lesson of losing someone under her care.

Teal'C had fired on his former friends and comrades, killing as many as he could.

Daniel Jackson wept through a drugged sleep in Medical.

He himself had accomplished nothing, not even a glimpse of his foster son.

On M'kwethet, the ones not Chosen for the tribute slept safe in their own homes, comfortable, secure—at least until the next Choosing.

And at least one young woman now held the keys to the universe.

O'Neill stared blindly at the neatly blocked report, and thought of all that, and wondered:

Was it worth it?